NORTH INDIAN RIVER COUNTY LIBRARY

P9-BYZ-495

GK Hall
3095

NORTH INDIAN RIVER COUNTY LIBRARY
1001 SEBASTIAN BLVD. (C.R. 512)
SEBASTIAN, FLORIDA 32958
PHONE: (772) 589-1355

IMPULSE

***Also by Nora Roberts
in Large Print:***

Birthright
Chesapeake Blue
Cordina's Crown Jewel
Face the Fire
From This Day
Key of Knowledge
Key of Light
Key of Valor
Lawless
Loving Jack
Night Moves
Search for Love
Sullivan's Woman
Time and Again

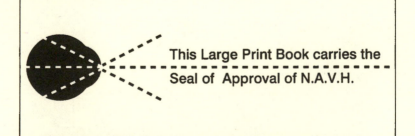

This Large Print Book carries the
Seal of Approval of N.A.V.H.

IMPULSE

Nora Roberts

Thorndike Press • Waterville, Maine

NORTH INDIAN RIVER COUNTY LIBRARY

Copyright © 1989 by Nora Roberts

All rights reserved.

All the characters in this book are fictitious. Any resemblance to actual persons, living or dead, is purely coincidental.

Published in 2004 by arrangement with Harlequin Books S.A.

Thorndike Press® Large Print Romance.

The tree indicium is a trademark of Thorndike Press.

The text of this Large Print edition is unabridged. Other aspects of the book may vary from the original edition.

Set in 16 pt. Plantin by Ramona Watson.

Printed in the United States on permanent paper.

Library of Congress Cataloging-in-Publication Data

Roberts, Nora.
    Impulse / Nora Roberts.
      p. cm.
    ISBN 0-7862-6538-8 (lg. print : hc : alk. paper)
    1. Americans — Greece — Fiction. 2. Women
travelers — Fiction. 3. Greece — Fiction. 4. Large
type books. I. Title.
PS3568.O243I47 2004
813′.54—dc22   2004045997

IMPULSE

National Association for Visual...

National Association for Visually Handicapped
---------------------- *serving the partially seeing*

As the Founder/CEO of NAVH, the only national health agency solely devoted to those who, although not totally blind, have an eye disease which could lead to serious visual impairment, I am pleased to recognize Thorndike Press* as one of the leading publishers in the large print field.

Founded in 1954 in San Francisco to prepare large print textbooks for partially seeing children, NAVH became the pioneer and standard setting agency in the preparation of large type.

Today, those publishers who meet our standards carry the prestigious "Seal of Approval" indicating high quality large print. We are delighted that Thorndike Press is one of the publishers whose titles meet these standards. We are also pleased to recognize the significant contribution Thorndike Press is making in this important and growing field.

Lorraine H. Marchi, L.H.D.
Founder/CEO
NAVH

* Thorndike Press encompasses the following imprints: Thorndike, Wheeler, Walker and Large Print Press.

Summer

Four years ago this month, I was married. When my soon-to-be husband and I were discussing plans for our honeymoon, there was one place that kept coming to my mind.

Greece. For as long as I can remember, I've dreamed of going to Greece, cruising the Aegean, imagining Adonis and Apollo and Aphrodite. I could picture myself walking near the Acropolis or sitting in a seaside café drinking ouzo. I wanted to walk in an olive grove and see wild goats. To me, Greece has always been one of the most romantic and exotic places in the world.

Well, things didn't work out. For the life of me, I can't exactly recall the reasons we changed our plans and headed to the resorts of Cancun and Cozumel on the Caribbean coast of Mexico. But it was all for the best. Right after we made our new plans, ordered tickets and reserved a hotel, the TWA flight out of Athens was hijacked.

We did have a wonderful time in Mexico. Blue water, gorgeous flowers, exotic music. Instead of Greek gods, I imagined ancient

Mayans. We didn't cruise the Aegean, but we snorkeled in the warm, clear Caribbean. I don't remember a single day when the sun didn't shine and the birds didn't sing. Of course, I was on my honeymoon.

We listened to mariachis and danced in the moonlight in the square in the village. We toured the ruins in Tulum, then swam in a lagoon called X-ha. That's where my new husband lost the keys to our rental car.

You don't always think of yourself as a foreigner, even in a foreign country, until you're faced with the language barrier. I could ask important things, like "How much does this cost?" and "Where's the rest room?" But I didn't have a clue how to explain that we'd lost the keys to our car somewhere in the lagoon and our hotel was an hour away.

But, like a true hero, my husband dived back in. The sunscreen had worn off and lunch was only a fond memory when he found them. But find them he did. I guess the gods look out for honeymooners.

Four years later and he's still my hero. From time to time we toy with the idea of that trip to Greece. I still hope to see Mount Olympus and walk in an olive grove. In the meantime, I went there in my imagination with Rebecca and Stephen. I hope you enjoy the trip as much as I did.

Chapter One

She knew it was crazy. That was what she liked best about it. It was crazy, ridiculous, impractical and totally out of character. And she was having the time of her life. From the balcony of her hotel suite Rebecca could see the sweep of the beach, the glorious blue of the Ionian Sea, blushed now with streaks of rose from the setting sun.

Corfu. Even the name sounded mysterious, exciting, glamorous. And she was here, really here. Practical, steady-as-a-rock Rebecca Malone, who had never traveled more than five hundred miles from Philadelphia, was in Greece. Not just in Greece, she thought with a grin, but on the exotic island of Corfu, in one of the most exclusive resorts in Europe.

First-class, she thought as she leaned out to let the sweet breeze ruffle over her face. As long as it lasted, she was going first-class.

Her boss had thought she was suffering from temporary insanity. Edwin McDowell of McDowell, Jableki and Kline was never going to understand why a promising young CPA would resign from her position with one of the top accounting firms in Philadelphia. She'd made a good salary, she'd enjoyed excellent benefits, and she'd even had a small window in her office.

Friends and associates had wondered if she'd suffered a breakdown. After all, it wasn't normal, and it certainly wasn't Rebecca's style to quit a solid, well-paying job without the promise of a better one.

But she'd given her two weeks' notice, cleared out her desk and had cheerfully walked out into the world of the unemployed.

When she'd sold her condo and then in one frantic week, auctioned off every possession she owned — every stick of furniture, every pot and pan and appliance — they'd been certain she'd gone over the edge.

Rebecca had never felt saner.

She owned nothing that didn't fit in a suitcase. She no longer had any tax-deferred investments or retirement plans. She'd cashed in her certificates of deposit, and the home entertainment center she'd thought she couldn't live without was now gracing someone else's home.

It had been more than six weeks since she'd even looked at an adding machine.

For the first — and perhaps the only — time in her life, she was totally free. There were no responsibilities, no pressures, no hurried gulps of cold coffee. She hadn't packed an alarm clock. She no longer owned one. Crazy? No. Rebecca shook her head and laughed into the breeze. For as long as it lasted, she was going to grab life with both hands and see what it had to offer.

Aunt Jeannie's death had been her turning point. It had come so suddenly, so unexpectedly, leaving Rebecca without any family. Aunt Jeannie had worked hard for most of her sixty-five years, always punctual, always responsible. Her position as head librarian had been her whole life. She'd never missed a day, never failed to do her duty. Her bills had been paid on time. Her promises had always been kept.

More than once Rebecca had been told she took after her mother's older sister. She was twenty-four, but she was — had been — as solid and sturdy as her maiden aunt. Two months into retirement, two months after dear Aunt Jeannie began to make plans to travel, to enjoy the rewards she'd worked so hard to earn, she was gone.

After Rebecca's grief had come the

anger, then the frustration, then slowly, the realization that she was traveling the same straight road. She worked, she slept, she fixed well-balanced meals that she ate alone. She had a small circle of friends who knew she could be counted on in a crisis. Rebecca would always find the best and most practical answer. Rebecca would never drop her own problems in your lap — because she didn't have any. Rebecca, bless her, was a port in any storm.

She hated it, and she'd begun to hate herself. She had to do something.

And she was doing it.

It wasn't running away as much as it was breaking free. All her life she'd done what was expected of her and tried to make as few waves as possible while doing it. All through school a crushing shyness had kept her more comfortable with her books than with other teenagers. In college a need to succeed and justify her aunt's faith had locked her tightly into her studies.

She had always been good with figures — logical, thorough, patient. It had been easy, perhaps too easy, to pour herself into that one area, because there, and really only there, had she felt confident.

Now she was going to discover Rebecca Malone. In the weeks or months of freedom she had, she wanted to learn everything there was to know about the woman within. Perhaps there wasn't a butterfly inside the cocoon she'd wrapped herself in so comfortably, but whatever she found — whoever she found — Rebecca hoped she would enjoy her, like her, perhaps even respect her.

When the money ran out, she'd get another job and go back to being plain, practical Rebecca. Until that time she was rich, rootless and ready for surprises.

She was also hungry.

Stephen saw her the moment she entered the restaurant. It wasn't that she was particularly striking. Beautiful women passed through the world every day and they usually warranted a glance. But there was something about the way this one walked, as if she were ready for anything, even looking forward to it. He stopped, and because business was slow at this hour he took a second, longer look.

She was tall for a woman, and more angular than slender. Her skin was pale, and that made him think she had only just arrived at the resort or was shy of the sun. The white sundress that left her shoulders and back bare accented the lack of color and gave dramatic contrast to her short cap of raven hair.

She paused, then seemed to take a deep breath. Stephen could almost hear her satisfied sigh. Then she smiled at the headwaiter, and followed him to her table, tossing her head back, so that her hair, which she wore arrow-straight, swung away from her chin.

A nice face, Stephen concluded. Bright, intelligent, eager. Especially the eyes. They were pale, an almost translucent gray. But there was nothing pale in their expression. She smiled at the waiter again, then laughed and looked around the restaurant. She looked as if she'd never been happier in her life.

She saw him. When Rebecca's gaze first skimmed over the man leaning against the bar, her automatic shyness kicked in and had her looking away. Attractive men had stared at her before — though it wasn't exactly a daily event. She'd never been able to handle it with the aplomb — or even cynicism — of most of her contemporaries. To cover her momentary embarrassment, she lifted her menu.

He hadn't meant to linger more than a few moments longer, but the impulse came suddenly. Stephen flicked a hand at the waiter and had him scurrying over, nodding quickly at Stephen's murmured request and hurrying off. When he returned it was to deliver a bottle of champagne to Rebecca's table.

"Compliments of Mr. Nickodemus."

"Oh." Rebecca followed the waiter's gaze over to the man by the bar. "Well, I —" She brought herself up short before she could stammer. A sophisticated woman wouldn't stutter over a gift of champagne, she reminded herself. She'd accept it graciously, with dignity. And maybe — if she wasn't a complete fool — she'd relax enough to flirt with the man who offered it.

Stephen watched the expressions pass across her face. Fascinating, he mused, and realized that the vague boredom he'd been feeling had vanished. When she lifted her head and smiled at him, he had no idea that her heart was pounding. He saw only a casual invitation, and he answered it.

He wasn't just attractive, Rebecca realized as he crossed to her table. He was gorgeous. Eye-popping, mouth-dropping gorgeous. She had an image of Apollo and ancient Greek warriors. Thick blond hair streaked by the sun fell over the collar of his shirt. Smooth, bronzed skin was marred — and somehow enhanced — by a

15

faint scar under his jawline. A strong jaw, she thought. A strong face, with the darkest, deepest blue eyes she'd ever seen.

"Good evening, I'm Stephen Nickodemus." His voice wasn't accented, it was rounded, rich. He might have come from anywhere. Perhaps it was that, more than anything else, that intrigued her.

Lecturing herself on poise and image, she lifted her hand. "Hello. I'm Rebecca, Rebecca Malone." She felt a quick flutter when he brushed his lips over her knuckles. Feeling foolish, she drew her hand away and balled it in her lap. "Thank you for the champagne."

"It seemed to suit your mood." He studied her, wondering why he was getting such a mix of signals. "You are by yourself?"

"Yes." Perhaps it was a mistake to admit it, but if she was going to live life to the fullest she had to take some risks. The restaurant wasn't crowded, but they were hardly alone. Take the plunge, she told herself, and tried another smile. "The least I can do is offer you a glass."

Stephen took the seat across from her, brushing the waiter aside to pour the wine himself. "You are American?"

"It shows."

"No. Actually, I thought you were French until you spoke."

"Did you?" That pleased her. "I've just come from Paris." She had to force herself not to touch her hair.

She'd had it cut, with trepidation and delight, in a French salon.

Stephen touched his glass to hers. Her eyes bubbled with life as cheerfully as the wine. "Business?"

"No, just pleasure." What a marvelous word, she thought. *Pleasure.* "It's a wonderful city."

"Yes. Do you go often?"

Rebecca smiled into her glass. "Not often enough. Do you?"

"From time to time."

She nearly sighed at that. Imagine anyone speaking of going to Paris "from time to time." "I nearly stayed longer, but I'd promised myself Greece."

So she was alone, restless, and on the move. Perhaps that was why she had appealed to him, because he was, too. "Is Corfu your first stop?"

"Yes." She sipped at her drink. A part of her still believed it was all a dream. Greece, champagne, the man. "It's beautiful. Much more beautiful than I imagined it could be."

"It's your first trip, then?" He couldn't have said why that pleased him. "How long do you stay?"

"As long as I like." She grinned, savoring the feeling of freedom. "And you?"

He lifted his glass. "Longer, I think, than I had planned." When the waiter appeared at his side, Stephen handed over the menu, then spoke to him in soft, quick Greek. "If you don't object, I'd like to guide you through your first meal on the island."

The old Rebecca would have been too nervous to sit through a meal with a stranger. The new Rebecca took a second, deeper sip of champagne. "I'd love it. Thank you."

It was easy. Easy to sit, to laugh, to sample new and exotic tastes. She forgot that he was a stranger, forgot that the world she was living in now was only temporary. They didn't speak of anything important — only of Paris, and the weather, and the wine. Still, she was sure it was the most interesting conversation of her life. He looked at her when he spoke to her, looked at her as though he were delighted to spend an hour talking of nothing. The last man she'd had dinner with had wanted her to give him a discount when she did his taxes.

Stephen wasn't asking her for anything more than her company for dinner. When he looked at her it seemed unlikely that he'd care if she knew how to fill out Schedule C.

When he suggested a walk along the beach, she agreed without a qualm. What better way to end an evening than a walk in the moonlight?

"I was looking out at this from my window just before dinner." Rebecca stepped out of her shoes, then dangled them from her fingers as she walked. "I didn't think it could look more beautiful than it did at sunset."

"The sea changes, like a woman, in the light." He paused to touch a flame to the end of a slim cigar. "So men are drawn to her."

"Are you? Drawn to the sea?"

"I've spent my time on her. I fished in these waters as a boy."

She'd learned at dinner that he'd grown up traveling the islands with his father. "It must have been exciting, moving from place to place, seeing new things almost every day."

He shrugged. He'd never been sure whether the restlessness had been born in him or had been a product of his upbringing. "It had its moments."

"I love to travel." Laughing, she tossed her shoes aside, then stepped into the surf. The champagne was making her head swim and the moonlight felt as soft as rain. "I adore it." She laughed again when the spray washed up to dampen her skirts. The Ionian Sea. She was standing in it. "On a night like this I think I'll never go home."

She looked so vibrant, so alive, standing in the surf with her white skirts billowing. "Where's home?"

She glanced over her shoulder. The flirtatious look was totally unplanned and completely devastating. "I haven't decided. I want to swim." On impulse, she dived into the surf.

Stephen's heart stopped when she disappeared. He'd already kicked off his shoes and started forward when she rose up again. For a second time, his heart stopped.

She was laughing, her face lifted to the moonlight. Water cascaded from her hair, from her skin. The drops that clung to her were the only jewels she wore. Beautiful? No, she wasn't beautiful. She was electric.

"It's wonderful. Cool and soft and wonderful."

With a shake of his head, he stepped in far enough to take her hand and pull her toward shore. She was a little mad, perhaps, but engagingly so. "Are you always so impulsive?"

"I'm working on it. Aren't you?" She combed her hand through her dripping hair. "Or do you always send champagne to strange women?"

"Either way I answer that could be trouble. Here." He shrugged out of his jacket and draped it over her shoulders. Unframed, washed clean, her face glowed in the moonlight. There was a graceful kind of strength in it, to the sweep of cheekbone, the slightly pointed chin. Delicate — except for the eyes. One look there showed power, a power that was still. "You're irresistible, Rebecca."

She stared at him, confused all over again, as he gathered the neck of the jacket close around her throat. "I'm wet," she managed.

"And beautiful." With his hands still on the jacket, he brought her toward him. "And fascinating."

That made her laugh again. "I don't think so, but thanks. I'm glad you sent me the champagne and guided me through my first meal." Her nerves began to jangle. His eyes stayed on hers, journeying only once to her mouth, which was still damp from the sea. Their bodies were close, close enough to brush. Rebecca began to shiver, and she knew it had nothing to do with wet clothes and the breeze.

"I should go in . . . change my dress."

There was something about her. The impulsiveness, the easy flirtatiousness, hid an unmistakable innocence that baffled and attracted him. Whatever it was, he wanted more.

"I'll see you again."

"Yes." She prayed for her heartbeat to slow. "It's not a very big island."

He smiled at that, slowly. She felt, with a mixture of relief and regret, the relaxation of his hands. "Tomorrow. I have business early. I'll be done by eleven, if that suits you. I'll show you Corfu."

"All right." Better judgment and nerves be damned. She wanted to go with him. "I'll meet you in the lobby." Carefully, because she suddenly wasn't sure she could manage it, she stepped back. Moonlight silhouetted him against the sea. "Good night, Stephen."

She forgot to be sophisticated and dashed toward the hotel.

He watched her go. She puzzled him, puzzled him as no woman had since he'd been a boy and too young to understand

that a woman was not meant to be understood. And he wanted her. That wasn't
new, but the desire had come with surprising speed and surprising force.

Rebecca Malone might have started out
as an impulse, but she was now a mystery.
One he intended to solve. With a little
laugh, he bent to scoop up the shoes she'd
forgotten. He hadn't felt quite so alive in
months.

Chapter Two

Stephen wasn't the kind of man who re-arranged his schedule to spend the day with a woman. Especially a woman he barely knew. He was a wealthy man, but he was also a busy man, driven by both pride and ambition to maintain a high level of involvement in all his projects. He shouldered responsibility well and had learned to enjoy the benefits of hard work and dedication.

His time on Corfu wasn't free — or rather hadn't been planned as free. Mixing business and pleasure wasn't his style. He pursued both, separately, with utter concentration. Yet he found himself juggling appointments, meetings, conference calls, in order to have the afternoon open for Rebecca.

He supposed any man would want to get to know a woman who flirted easily over a champagne flute one moment and dived fully dressed into the sea the next.

"I've postponed your meeting with Theoharis until five-thirty this evening." Stephen's secretary scribbled on a notepad she had resting on her lap. "He will meet you for early cocktails in the suite. I've arranged for hors d'oeuvres and a bottle of ouzo."

"Always efficient, Elana."

She smiled and tucked a fall of dark hair behind her ear. "I try."

When Stephen rose to pace to the window, she folded her hands and waited. She had worked for him for five years, she admired his energy and his business acumen, and — fortunately for both of them — had long since gotten over an early crush. There was often speculation about their personal relationship, but though he could be friendly — even kind when it suited him — with Stephen, business was business.

"Contact Mithos in Athens. Have him telex that report by the end of the day. And I want to hear from Lereau by five, Paris time."

"Shall I call and give him a nudge?"

"If you think it's necessary." Restless, he dug his hands in his pockets. Where had this sudden discontent come from? he wondered. He was wealthy, successful, and free, as always, to move from place to place. As he stared out at the sea, he remembered the scent of Rebecca's skin.

"Send flowers to Rebecca Malone's suite. Wildflowers, nothing formal. This afternoon."

Elana made a note, hoping she'd get a look at this Rebecca Malone before long. She had already heard through the grapevine that Stephen had had dinner with an American woman. "And the card?"

He wasn't a man for poetry. "Just my name."

"Anything else?"

"Yes." He turned and offered her a half smile. "Take some time off. Go to the beach."

Pad in hand, she rose. "I'll be sure to work it in. Enjoy your afternoon, Stephen."

He intended to. As she left him, Stephen glanced at his watch. It was fifteen minutes before eleven. There was work he could do to fill in the time, a quick call that could be made. Instead, he picked up Rebecca's shoes.

After three tries, Rebecca settled on an outfit. She didn't have an abundance of clothes, because she'd preferred to spend her funds on travel. But she had splurged here and there on her route through Europe. No tidy CPA suits, she thought as she tied a vivid fuchsia sash at the waist of her sapphire-colored cotton pants. No sensible shoes or pastel blouses. The last shock of color came from a primrose-hued blouse cut generously to layer over a skinny tank top in the same shade as the slacks.

The combination delighted her, if only because her firm had preferred quiet colors and clean lines.

She had no idea where she was going, and she didn't care.

It was a beautiful day, even though she'd awoken with a dull headache from the champagne, and the disorientation that went with it. A light, early breakfast on her terrace and a quick dip in the sea had cleared both away. She still had trouble believing that she could lounge through a morning as she pleased — and that she'd spent the evening with a man she'd just met.

Aunt Jeannie would have tut-tutted and reminded her of the dangers of being a woman alone. Some of her friends would have been shocked, others envious. But they would all have been astonished that steady Rebecca had strolled in the moonlight with a gorgeous man with a scar on his jawline and eyes like velvet.

If she hadn't had his jacket as proof, she

might have thought she'd dreamed it. There had never been anything wrong with her imagination — just the application of it. Often she'd pictured herself in an exotic place with an exotic man, with moonlight and music. Imagined herself, she remembered. And then she'd turned on her calculator and gotten down to business.

But she hadn't dreamed this. She could still remember the giddy, half-terrified feeling that had swarmed through her when he'd gathered her close. When his mouth had been only an inch from hers and the sea and the champagne had roared in her head.

What if he had kissed her? What tastes would she have found? Rich, strong ones, she mused, almost able to savor them as she traced a fingertip over her lips. After just one evening she was absolutely certain there would be nothing lukewarm about Stephen Nickodemus. She wasn't nearly so certain about Rebecca.

She probably would have fumbled and blushed and stammered. With a shake of her head, she pulled a brush through her hair. Exciting men didn't tumble all over themselves to kiss neat, practical-minded women.

But he'd asked to see her again.

Rebecca wasn't certain whether she was disappointed or relieved that he hadn't pressed his advantage and kissed her. She'd been kissed before, held before, of course. But she had a feeling — a very definite feeling — that it wouldn't be the same with Stephen. He might make her want more, offer more, than she had with any other man.

Crossing bridges too soon, she decided as she checked the contents of her big straw bag. She wasn't going to have an affair with him, or with anyone. Even the new, improved Rebecca Malone wasn't the type for a casual affair. But maybe — She caught her lower lip between her teeth. If the time was right she might have a romance she'd remember long after she left Greece.

For now, she was ready, but it was much too early to go down. It would hardly make her look like a well-traveled woman of the world if she popped down to the lobby and paced for ten minutes. This was her fantasy, after all. She didn't want him to think she was inexperienced and overeager.

Only the knock on the door prevented her from changing her mind about her outfit one more time.

"Hello." Stephen studied her for a moment, unsmiling. He'd nearly been certain

29

he'd exaggerated, but she was just as vibrant, just as exciting, in the morning as she had been in the moonlight. He held out her shoes. "I thought you might need these."

She laughed, remembering her impulsive dunk in the sea. "I didn't realize I'd left them on the beach. Come in a minute." With a neatness ingrained in her from childhood, she turned to take them to the bedroom closet. "I'm ready to go if you are."

Stephen lifted a brow. He preferred promptness, but he never expected it in anyone but a business associate. "I've got a Jeep waiting. Some of the roads are rough."

"Sounds great." Rebecca came out again, carrying her bag and a flat-brimmed straw hat. She handed Stephen his jacket, neatly folded. "I forgot to give this back to you last night." Should she offer to have it cleaned? she wondered when he only continued to look at her. Fiddling with the strap of her bag, she decided against it. "Does taking pictures bother you?"

"No, why?"

"Good, because I take lots of them. I can't seem to stop myself."

She wasn't kidding. As Stephen drove up

into the hills, she took shots of everything. Sheep, tomato plants, olive groves and straggly sage. He stopped so that she could walk out near the edge of a cliff and look down at a small village huddled near the sea.

She wouldn't be able to capture it on film; she wasn't clever enough. But she knew she'd never forget that light, so pure, so clear, or the contrast between the orange tiled roofs and the low white-washed walls and the deep, dangerous blue of the water that flung itself against the weathered rock that rose into harsh crags. A stork, legs tucked, glided over the water, where fishing boats bobbed.

There were nets drying on the beach and children playing. Flowers bloomed and tangled where the wind had planted them, more spectacular than any planned arrangement could ever be.

"It's beautiful." Her throat tightened with emotion, and with a longing she couldn't have defined. "So calm. You imagine women baking black bread and the men coming home smelling of fish and the sea. It looks as though it hasn't changed in a hundred years."

"Very little." He glanced down himself, surprised and more than a little pleased that she would be touched by something so simple. "We cling to antiquity."

"I haven't seen the Acropolis yet, but I don't think it could be any more spectacular than this." She lifted her face, delighted by the way the wind whipped at it. Here, high above the sea, she absorbed everything — the salty, rough-edged bite of the wind, the clarity of color and sound, and the man beside her. Letting her camera dangle from its strap, she turned to him. "I haven't thanked you for taking the time to show me all of this."

He took her hand, not to raise it to his lips, just to hold it. It was a link he hadn't known he wanted. "I'm enjoying seeing the familiar through someone else's eyes. Your eyes."

Suddenly the edge of the cliff seemed too close, the sun too hot. Could he do that just by touching her? With an effort, Rebecca smiled, keeping her voice light. "If you ever come to Philadelphia, I'll do the same for you."

It was odd. She'd looked almost frightened for a moment. Fragile and frightened. Stephen had always carefully avoided women who were easily bruised. "I'll consider that a promise."

They continued to drive, over roads that

jarred and climbed and twisted. She saw her first of the *agrimi*, the wild goat of Greece, and the rocky pastures dotted with sturdy sheep. And everywhere, rich and defiant, was the intense color of flowers.

He didn't complain when she asked him to stop so that she could snap pictures of tiny blue star blossoms that pushed their way through cracks in the rock. He listened to her delight as she framed a thick, thorny stem topped with a ragged yellow flower. It made him realize, and regret, that it had been years since he'd taken the time to look closely at the small, vital things that grew around him.

He looked now, at Rebecca standing in the sunlight, her hat fluttering around her face and her laugh dancing on the air.

Often the road clung to cliffs that plunged dizzily into the sea. Rebecca, who was too timid to fight rush-hour traffic, found it exhilarating.

She felt almost like another person. She *was* another person, she thought, laughing as she held on to her hat to keep the wind from snatching it away.

"I love it!" she shouted over the wind and the noise of the engine. "It's wild and old and incredible. Like no place I've ever been."

Still laughing, she lifted her camera and snapped his picture as he drove. He wore sunglasses with amber lenses and had a cigar clamped between his teeth. The wind blew through his hair and chased the smoke behind them. He stopped the Jeep, took the camera and snapped a picture of her in turn.

"Hungry?"

She dragged her tousled hair back from her face. "Starving."

He leaned over to open her door. A current passed through her, sharp and electric, strong enough to make him pause with his arm across her body and his face close to hers. It was there again, he thought as he waited and watched. The awareness, ripe and seductive. And the innocence, as alluring as it was contradictory. In a test — a test for both of them — he lifted a hand to stroke her cheek. It was as soft as her scent.

"Are you afraid of me, Rebecca?"

"No." That was true; she was nearly sure of it. "Should I be?"

He didn't smile. Through the amber lenses she saw that his eyes were very intense. "I'm not entirely sure." When he pulled away he heard her release an unsteady breath. He wasn't feeling completely steady himself. "We'll have to walk a little first."

Confused, her mind churning, she stepped out onto the dirt path. A woman on a simple date didn't tremble every time a man got close, Rebecca told herself as Stephen lifted the picnic basket out of the back. She was behaving like a teenager, not a grown woman.

Troubled by his own thoughts, Stephen stopped beside her. He hesitated, then held out a hand. It felt good, simply good, when she put hers in it.

They walked through an olive grove in a companionable silence while the sun streamed down on dusty leaves and rocky ground. There was no sound of the sea here, but when the wind was right she could hear the screech of a gull far away. The island was small, but here it seemed uninhabited.

"I haven't had a picnic in years." Rebecca spread the cloth. "And never in an olive grove." She glanced around, wanting to remember every leaf and pebble. "Are we trespassing?"

"No." Stephen took a bottle of white wine from the basket. Rebecca left him to it and started rummaging in search of food.

"Do you know the owner?"

"I'm the owner." He drew the cork with a gentle pop.

"Oh." She looked around again. It should have occurred to her that he would own something impressive, different, exciting. "It sounds romantic. Owning an olive grove."

He lifted a brow. He owned a number of them, but he had never thought of them as romantic. They were simply profitable. He offered her a glass, then tapped it with his own. "To romance, then."

She swept down her lashes, battling shyness. To Stephen, the gesture was only provocative. "I hope you're hungry," she began, knowing she was talking too fast. "It all looks wonderful." She took a quick sip of wine to ease her dry throat, then set it aside to finish unpacking the basket.

There were sweet black olives as big as a man's thumb, and there was a huge slab of sharp cheese. There were cold lamb and hunks of bread, and fruit so fresh it could have been just plucked from the stem.

Gradually she began to relax again.

"You've told me very little about yourself." Stephen topped off her wine and watched her bite into a ripe red plum. "I know little more than that you come from

36

Philadelphia and enjoy traveling."

What could she tell him? A man like him was bound to be bored with the life story of the painfully ordinary Rebecca Malone. Lies had never come easily to her, so she skirted between fact and fiction. "There's little more. I grew up in Philadelphia. I lost both of my parents when I was a teenager, and I lived with my aunt Jeannie. She was very dear, and she made the loss bearable."

"It's painful." He flicked his lighter at the end of a cigar, remembering not only the pain, but also the fury he had felt when his father had died and left him orphaned at sixteen. "It steals childhood."

"Yes." So he understood that. It made her feel close to him, close and comfortable. "Maybe that's why I like to travel. Every time you see a new place you can be a child again."

"So you don't look for roots?"

She glanced at him then. He was leaning back against the trunk of a tree, smoking lazily, watching carefully. "I don't know what I'm looking for."

"Is there a man?"

She moved her shoulders, determined not to be embarrassed. "No."

He took her hand, drawing her closer. "No one?"

"No, I . . ." She wasn't certain what she would have said, but could say nothing at all when he turned her palm upward and pressed his lips to its center. She felt the fire burst there, in her hand, then race everywhere.

"You're very responsive, Rebecca." He lowered her hand but kept it in his. He could feel the heat, but he wasn't sure whether it had sprung to her skin or to his own. "If there's no one, the men in your Philadelphia must be very slow."

"I've been too . . . busy."

His lips curved at that. There was a tremor in her voice, and there was passion in her eyes. "Busy?"

"Yes." Afraid she'd make a fool of herself, she drew her hand back. "This was wonderful." Trying to calm herself, she pushed a hand through her hair. "You know what I need?"

"No. Tell me."

"Another picture." She sprang to her feet and, steadier, grinned. "A memento of my first picnic in an olive grove. Let's see . . . you can stand right over there. The sun's good in front of that tree, and I should be able to frame in that section of the grove."

Amused, Stephen tapped out his cigar.

"How much more film do you have?"

"This is the last roll — but I have scads back at the hotel." She flicked him a quick laughing glance. "I warned you."

"So you did." Competent hands, he thought as he watched her focus and adjust. He hadn't realized he could be as attracted to competence as he was to beauty. She mumbled to herself, tossing her head back so that her hair swung, then settled. His stomach tightened without warning.

Good God, he wanted her. She'd done nothing to make him burn and strain this way. He couldn't accuse her of taunting or teasing, and yet . . . he felt taunted. He felt teased. For the first time in his life he felt totally seduced by a woman who had done nothing more than give him a few smiles and a little companionship.

Even now she was chattering away as she secured her camera to the limb of a tree. Talking easily, as though they were just friends, as though she felt nothing more than a light, unimportant affection. But he'd seen it. Stephen felt his blood heat as he remembered the quick flash of arousal he'd seen on her face. He'd see it again. And more.

"I'm going to set the timer," Rebecca went on, blissfully unaware of Stephen's thoughts. "All you have to do is stand there. Once I get this damn thing set, I'm going to run over so it'll take one of both — There." She interrupted herself, crossed her fingers and ran to Stephen's side in a dash. "Unless I messed up, it'll snap all by itself in —"

The rest of the words slid down her throat as he crushed her against him and captured her mouth.

Chapter Three

Heat. Light. Speed. Rebecca felt them, felt each separate, distinct sensation. Urgency. Demand. Impatience. She tasted them, as clearly as wild honey, on his lips. Though she'd never experienced it, she had known exactly what it would be like to be with him, mouth to mouth and need to need.

In an instant the world had narrowed from what could be seen and understood to a pure, seamless blanket of emotion. It cloaked her, not softly, not in comfort, but tightly, hotly, irresistibly. Caught between fear and delight, she lifted a hand to his cheek.

God, she was sweet. Even as he dragged her closer, aroused by the simplicity of her acceptance, he was struck by — disarmed by — her sweetness. There had been a hesitation, almost too brief to be measured, before her lips had parted beneath his. Parted, invited, accepted.

There was a sigh, so soft it could barely be heard, as she stroked her hands up his back to his shoulders. Curious, simple,

41

generous. A man could drown in such sweetness, fall prisoner to such pliancy. And be saved by it. Beneath the patterned shade of the olive tree, she gave him more than passion. She gave him hope.

Charmed, he murmured some careless Greek phrase lovers might exchange. The words meant nothing to her, but the sound of them on the still air, the feel of them stroking across her lips . . . seduction. Glorious seduction.

Pleasure burst in her blood, in her head, in her heart, thousands of tiny bubbles of it, until she was straining against him.

The quiet explosion rocked him. It tightened his chest, fuddled his mind. She fitted into his arms as if she'd been born for him. As if, somehow, they had known each other before, loved before, hungered before. Something seemed to erupt between them, something molten, powerful, dangerous. But it wasn't new. It was ancient, a whispering echo of ageless passions.

She began to tremble. How could this be so right, so familiar? It wasn't possible to feel safe and threatened at the same time. But she did. She clung to him while a dim, floating image danced through her head. She had kissed him before. Just like this. As her mind spun, she heard her own mindless murmurs answer his. As freely, as inescapably as the sun poured light, response flowed from her. She couldn't stop it. Frightened by her sudden loss of control, she struggled against him, against herself.

He slipped his hands up to her shoulders, but not to free her, to look at her. To look at how their coming together had changed her. It had changed him. Passion had made her eyes heavy, seductive. Fear had clouded them. Her lips were full, softened and parted by his. Her breath shivered through them. Under his hands he could feel the heat of her skin and the quick, involuntary trembling of her muscles.

No pretense here, he decided as he studied her. He was holding both innocence and delight in his hands.

"Stephen, I —"

"Again."

Then his face filled her vision and she was lost.

Differently. Should she have known that one man could hold one woman in so many different ways? That one man could kiss one woman with such stunning variety? There was gentleness now, as familiar and as novel as the urgency. His lips persuaded rather than demanded. They savored instead of devouring. Her surrender came as quietly, and as unmistakably, as her earlier passion. The trembling stopped; the fear vanished. With a complete trust that surprised them both, she leaned against him, giving.

More aroused by her serenity than by the storm that had come before, Stephen pulled back. He had to, or what had begun would finish without either of them saying a word. As he swore and pulled out a cigar, Rebecca placed a hand on the olive tree for support.

Moments, she thought. It had been only moments, and yet she felt as though years had passed, racing backward or forward, perhaps spinning in circles. In a place like this, with a man like this, what difference did it make what year it was? What century?

Half terrified, she lifted a hand to her lips. Despite her fear, they curved under her touch. She could still taste him. Still feel him. And nothing, nothing, would ever be quite the same again.

He stared out at the rough and dusty land he'd known as a boy, and beyond, to the stark, tumbling rocks where he and other wild things had climbed.

What was he doing with her? Furious with himself, he drew on the cigar. What was he feeling? It was new, and far from comfortable. And it was comfort he preferred, he reminded himself. Comfort and freedom. Bringing himself under control, he turned to her again, determined to treat what had happened as a man should — lightly.

She just stood there, with the sun and the shade falling over her. There was neither recrimination nor invitation in her eyes. She didn't flinch or step forward, but merely stood, watching him with the faintest of smiles, as if . . . As if, Stephen realized, she knew what questions he was asking himself — and the answers.

"It grows late."

She felt the ache and fought not to let it show on her face. "I guess you're right." She dragged a hand through her hair — it was the first sign of her agitation — then walked over to pick up her camera. "I should have a picture to remember all this by," she said, forcing brightness into her voice. Her breath caught when his fingers closed over her arm and whirled her around.

"Who are you?" he demanded. "What are you?"

"I don't know what you mean." The

emotion burst out before she could stop it. "I don't know what you want."

With one jerk he had her tumbling against him. "You know what I want."

Her heart was in her throat, beating wildly. She found it strange that it was not fear but desire that she felt. She hadn't known she was capable of feeling a need that was so unreasonable, so reckless. It was almost purifying to experience it, and to see it mirrored in his eyes.

"It takes more than one afternoon." Didn't it? Her voice rose as she tried to convince herself. "It takes more than a picnic and a walk in the moonlight for me."

"One moment the temptress, the next the outraged innocent. Do you do it to intrigue me, Rebecca?" She shook her head, and his fingers tightened. "It works," he murmured. "You've hardly been out of my mind since I first saw you. I want to make love with you, here, in the sun."

Color flooded her face, not because she was embarrassed, but because she could imagine it, perfectly. And then what? Carefully she leveled her breathing. Whatever impulses she had followed, whatever bridges she had burned, she still needed answers.

"No." It cost her to go against her own needs and say it. "Not when I'm unsure and you're angry." She took a deep breath and kept her eyes on him. "You're hurting me, Stephen. I don't think you mean to."

Slowly he released her arm. He was angry, furious, but not at her refusal. The anger stemmed from the need she pulled from him, a need that had come too fast and too strong for him to channel. "We'll go back."

Rebecca merely nodded, then knelt to gather the remains of the picnic.

He was a busy man, much too busy to brood about a woman he barely knew and didn't understand at all. That was what Stephen told himself. He had reports to read, calls to make and paperwork — which he had both a talent and a distaste for — to deal with. A couple of simple kisses weren't enough to take a man's mind off his work.

But there hadn't been anything simple about them. Disgusted, Stephen pushed away from his desk and wandered to the terrace doors. He'd left them open because the breeze, and the fragrances it brought, helped him forget he was obligated to be inside.

For days he'd worked his way through his responsibilities, trying to ignore the nagging itch at the back of his mind — the itch that was Rebecca. There was no reason for him to stay on Corfu. He could have handled his business in Athens, or Crete, or in London, for that matter. Still, he'd made no plans to leave, though he'd also made no attempt to approach her.

She . . . concerned him, he decided. To be drawn to an attractive woman was as natural as breathing. To have the attraction cause discomfort, confusion, even annoyance was anything but natural. A taste of her hadn't been enough. Yet he hesitated.

She was . . . mysterious. Perhaps that was why he couldn't push her from his mind. On the surface she appeared to be an attractive, free-spirited woman who grabbed life with both hands. Yet there were undercurrents. The hints of innocence, of shyness. The sweetness. The complexity of her kept him wondering, thinking, imagining.

Perhaps that was her trick. Women had them . . . were entitled to them. It was a waste of time to begrudge them their illusions and their feminine magic. More than a waste of time, it was foolish, when a man could enjoy the benefits. But there was more, and somehow less, to Rebecca than innate feminine magic.

When he had kissed her, though it had been the first time, it had been like coming back to a lover, to a love, after a painful separation. When his lips had found hers, something had filled him. A heat, an impatience, a knowledge.

He knew her, knew more than her name and her background and the color of her eyes. He knew all of her. Yet he knew nothing.

Fantasies, he told himself. He didn't have time for them. Leaning a hip against the railing, he lit a cigar and watched the sea.

As always, it pulled at him, bringing back memories of a childhood that had been careless and too short. There were times, rare times, when he allowed himself to regret. Times when the sun was a white flash of heat and the water was blue and endless. His father had taught him a great deal. How to fish, how to see both beauty and excitement in new places, how to drink like a man.

Fifteen years, Stephen thought, a smile ghosting around his mouth. He still missed him, missed the companionship, the robust laughter. They had been friends, as well as parent and child, with a bond as easy, and as strong, as any Stephen had ever known. But his father had died as he would have wanted to, at sea and in his prime.

He would have taken one look at Rebecca, rolled his eyes, kissed his fingers and urged his son to enjoy. But Stephen wasn't the boy he had once been. He was more cautious, more aware of consequences. If a man dived into the sea, he should know the depth and the currents.

Then he saw her, coming from the sea. Water ran down her body, glistening in the strong sun, sparkling against skin that had warmed in the last few days to a dusky gold. As he looked, as he wanted, he felt his muscles clench, one by one, shoulders, stomach, thighs. Without his being aware, his fingers tightened, snapping the cigar in two. He hadn't known that desire could arouse a reaction so akin to anger.

She stopped, and though he knew she was unaware of him, she might easily have been posing. To taunt, to tease, to invite. As drops of water slid down her, she stretched, lifting her face skyward. Her skimpy suit rested low over her boyish hips, shifted enticingly over the subtle curve of her breasts. At that moment, she was totally absorbed in her own pleasure and as unself-conscious as any young animal standing in the sun. Nothing had ever been so alluring.

Then, slowly, seductively, she combed her fingers through her hair, smiling, as if she enjoyed the wet, silky feel of it. Watching her, he felt the air back up and clog in his lungs. He could have murdered her for it, for making him want so unreasonably what he did not yet understand.

She plucked a long, mannish T-shirt from a straw bag and, after tugging it on, strolled barefoot into the hotel.

He stood there, waiting for the need to pass. But it built, layered with an ache that infuriated him and a longing that baffled him.

He should ignore her. Instinct warned him that if he didn't his life would never be the same. She was nothing more than a distraction, a momentary impulse he should resist. He should turn away, go back to work. He had commitments, obligations, and no time to waste on fantasies. With an oath, he tossed the broken cigar over the rail.

There were times, he thought, when a man had to trust in fate and dive in.

Chapter Four

Rebecca had hardly shut the door behind her before she turned back to answer the knock. The sun and the water had left her pleasantly tired, but all thoughts of a lazy catnap vanished when she saw Stephen.

He looked wonderful. Cool, a little windblown, intense. For days she'd wondered about him, wondered and wished. She felt her pulse skip and her lips curve just at the sight of him. With an effort, she kept her voice breezy.

"Hello. I wasn't sure you were still on the island."

It wasn't really a lie, she told herself. An offhand inquiry had assured her that Mr. Nickodemus hadn't checked out, but she hadn't actually seen him.

"I saw you come up from the beach."

"Oh." Unconsciously she tugged at the hem of her cover-up. To Stephen the small gesture was one more contradictory signal. "I can't seem to get enough of the sun and the sea. Would you like to come in?"

By way of an answer he stepped through and shut the door behind him. It made a very quiet, a very final sound. Rebecca's carefully built poise began to crumble. "I never thanked you for the flowers." She made a gesture indicating the vase near the window, then brought her hands back together and linked them in front of her. "They're still beautiful. I . . . I thought I might run into you, in the dining room, on the beach, or . . ." Her words trailed off when he lifted a hand to her hair.

"I've been busy." He watched her eyes, eyes that were as clear as rainwater, blur at the slight touch. "Business."

It was ridiculous, she knew, but she wasn't at all sure she could speak. "If you have to work, I doubt you could pick a more beautiful place."

He stepped closer. She smelled of the water and the sun. "You're enjoying the resort, and the island."

Her hand was in his now, caught lightly. It took only that to make her knees weak. "Yes, very much."

"Perhaps you'd like to see it from a different perspective." Deliberately, wanting to test them both, he lifted her hand to his lips. He grazed her knuckles — it was barely a whisper of contact — and felt the jolt. She felt it, and he could see that she did, so it couldn't just be his imagination. "Spend the day with me tomorrow on my boat."

"What?"

He smiled, delighted with her response. "Will you come with me?"

Anywhere. Astonished, she stepped back. "I haven't any plans."

"Good." He closed the distance between them again. Her hands fluttered up in flustered defense, then settled again when he made no attempt to touch her. "Then I'll make them for you. I'll come for you in the morning. Nine?"

A boat. He'd said something about a boat. Rebecca drew in a deep breath and tried to pull herself together. This wasn't like her — going off into daydreams, feeling weak-kneed, being flooded with waves of desire. And it felt wonderful.

"I'd like that." She gave him what she hoped was an easy woman-of-the-world smile.

"Until tomorrow, then." He started for the door, then turned, a hand on the knob. "Rebecca, don't forget your camera."

She waited until he'd closed the door before she spun in three quick circles.

★ ★ ★

When Stephen had said "boat," Rebecca had pictured a trim little cabin cruiser. Instead, she stepped onto the glossy mahogany deck of a streamlined hundred-foot yacht.

"You could live on this," Rebecca said, then wished she'd bitten her tongue. But he only laughed.

"I often do."

"Welcome aboard, sir," a white-uniformed man with a British accent said.

"Grady. This is my guest, Miss Malone."

"Ma'am." Grady's cool British reserve didn't flicker for an instant, but Rebecca felt herself being summed up.

"Cast off when you're ready." Stephen took Rebecca's arm. "Would you like a tour?"

"Yes." A yacht. She was on a yacht. It took all her willpower to keep her camera in the bag. "I'd love to see it all."

He took her below, through four elegantly appointed cabins. Her comment about living on board had been said impulsively, but she could see now that it could be done easily, even luxuriously.

Above there was a large glassed-in cabin in which one could stretch out comfortably, out of the sun, and watch the sea, whatever the weather. She had known that there were people who lived like this. Part of her job had been to research and calculate so that those who did paid the government as little as possible. But to be there, to see it, to be surrounded by it, was entirely different from adding figures on paper.

There was a masculine feel to the cabin, to the entire boat — leather, wood, muted colors. There were shelves filled with books and a fully stocked bar, as well as a stereo system.

"All the comforts of home," Rebecca murmured, but she'd noted that there were doors and panels that could be secured in case of rough weather. What would it be like to ride out a storm at sea, to watch the rain lash the windows and feel the deck heave?

She gave a quick gasp when she felt the floor move. Stephen took her arm again to steady her.

"We're under way." Curious, he turned her to face him. "Are you afraid of boats?"

"No." She could hardly admit that the biggest one she'd been on before this had been a two-passenger canoe at summer camp. "It just startled me." Under way, she thought as she prayed that her system would settle. It was such an exciting, adventurous word. "Can we go out on deck? I'd like to watch."

It was exciting. She felt it the moment the wind hit her face and rushed through her hair. At the rail, she leaned out, delighted to see the island shrink and the sea spread. Because she couldn't resist and he didn't laugh at her, she took half a dozen pictures as the boat sped away from land.

"It's better than flying," she decided. "You feel a part of it. Look." With a laugh, she pointed. "The birds are chasing us."

Stephen didn't bother to glance at the gulls that wheeled and called above the boat's wake. He preferred to watch the delight and excitement bloom on her face. "Do you always enjoy so completely?"

"Yes." She tossed her hair away from her face, only to have the wind rush it back again. With another laugh, she stretched back from the railing, her face lifted to the sun. "Oh, yes."

Irresistible. With his hands at her waist, he spun her toward him. It was like holding a live wire. The shock rippled from her to him, then back again. "Everything?" His fingers spread over her back and, with the slightest pressure, moved her forward until their thighs met.

"I don't know." Instinctively she braced her hands on his shoulders. "I haven't tried everything." But she wanted to. Held close, with the sound of the water and the wind, she wanted to. Without giving a thought to self-preservation, she leaned toward him.

He swore, lightly, under his breath. Rebecca jolted back as if he had shouted at her. Stephen caught her hand as he nodded to the steward, who had just approached with drinks. "Thank you, Victor. Just leave everything." His voice was smooth enough, but Rebecca felt the tension in his hand as he led her to a chair.

He probably thought she was a fool, she decided. All but tumbling into his arms every time he touched her. He was obviously a man of the world — and a kind man, she added as she sipped her mimosa. Not all powerful men spoke kindly to those who worked for them. Her lips curved, a little wryly, as she sipped again. She knew that firsthand.

His body was in turmoil. Stephen couldn't remember, even in his youth, having had a woman affect him so irrationally. He knew how to persuade, how to seduce — and always with finesse. But whenever he was around this woman for more than five minutes he felt like a stallion being spurred and curbed at the same time.

And he was fascinated. Fascinated by the ease with which she went into his arms, by the trust he saw when he looked down into her eyes. As he had in the olive grove, he found himself believing he'd looked into those eyes, those rainwater-clear eyes, a hundred times before.

Still churning, he took out a cigar. The thought was fanciful, but his desire was very real. If there couldn't be finesse, perhaps there could be candor.

"I want you, Rebecca."

She felt her heart stop, then start up again with slow, dull throbs. Carefully she took another sip, then cleared her throat. "I know." It amazed her, flattered her, terrified her.

She seemed so cool. He envied her. "Will you come with me, to my cabin?"

She looked at him then. Her heart and her head were giving very different answers. It sounded so easy, so . . . natural. If there was a man she could give herself to, wholly, he was with her now. Complications, what complications there were, were her own.

But no matter how far she had run from Philadelphia and her own strict upbringing, there were still lines she couldn't cross.

"I can't."

"Can't?" He lit his cigar, astonished that they were discussing making love as though it were as casual a choice as what dinner entrée to choose. "Or won't?"

She drew a breath. Her palms were damp on the glass, and she set it down. "Can't. I want to." Her eyes, huge and lake-pale, clung to his. "I very much want to, but . . ."

"But?"

"I know so little about you." She picked up her glass again because her empty hands tended to twist together. "Hardly more than your name, that you own an olive grove and like the sea. It's not enough."

"Then I'll tell you more."

She relaxed enough to smile. "I don't know what to ask."

He leaned back in his chair, the tension dissolving as quickly as it had built. She could do that to him with nothing more than a smile. He knew no one who could excite and solace with so little effort.

"Do you believe in fate, Rebecca? In something unexpected, even unlooked-for, often a small thing that completely and irrevocably changes one's life?"

She thought of her aunt's death and her own uncharacteristic decisions. "Yes. Yes, I do."

"Good." His gaze skimmed over her face, quickly, then more leisurely. "I'd nearly forgotten that I believe it, too. Then I saw you, sitting alone."

There were ways and ways to seduce, she was discovering. A look, a tone, could be every bit as devastating as a caress. She wanted him more in that moment than she had ever known she could want anything. To give herself time, and distance, she rose and walked to the rail.

Even her silence aroused him. She had said she knew too little about him. He knew even less of her. And he didn't care. It was dangerous, possibly even destructive, but he didn't care. As he watched her with the wind billowing her shirt and her hair he realized that he didn't give a damn about where she had come from, where she had been, what she had done.

When lightning strikes, it destroys, though it blazes with power. Rising, he went to her and stood, as she did, facing the sea.

"When I was young, very young," he began, "there was another moment that changed things. My father was a man for the water. He lived for it. Died for it." When he went on it was almost as if he were speaking to himself now, remembering. Rebecca turned her head to look at him. "I was ten or eleven. Everything was going well, the nets were full. My father and I were walking along the beach. He stopped, dipped his hand into the water, made a fist and opened it. 'You can't hold it,' he said to me. 'No matter how you try or how you love or how you sweat.' Then he dug into the sand. It was wet and clung together in his hand. 'But this,' he said, 'a man can hold.' We never spoke of it again. When my time came, I turned my back on the sea and held the land."

"It was right for you."

"Yes." He lifted a hand to catch at the ends of her hair. "It was right. Such big, quiet eyes you have, Rebecca," he murmured. "Have they seen enough, I wonder, to know what's right for you?"

"I guess I've been a little slow in starting to look." Her blood was pounding thickly. She would have stepped back, but he shifted so that she was trapped between him and the rail.

"You tremble when I touch you." He slid his hands up her arms, then down until their hands locked. "Have you any idea how exciting that is?"

Her chest tightened, diminishing her air even as the muscles in her legs went limp. "Stephen, I meant it when I said . . ." He brushed his lips gently over her temple. "I can't. I need to . . ." He feathered a kiss along her jawline, softly. "To think."

He felt her fingers go lax in his. She was suddenly fragile, outrageously vulnerable, irresistibly tempting. "When I kissed you the first time I gave you no choice." His lips trailed over her face, light as a whisper, circling, teasing, avoiding her mouth. "You have one now."

He was hardly touching her. A breath, a whisper, a mere promise of a touch. The slow, subtle passage of his lips over her skin couldn't have been called a kiss, could never have been called a demand. She had only to push away to end the torment. And the glory.

A choice? Had he told her she had a choice? "No, I don't," she murmured as she turned to find his lips with hers.

No choice, no past, no future. Only now. She felt the present, with all its needs and hungers, well up inside her. The kiss was instantly hot, instantly desperate. His heart pounded fast and hard against hers, thunderous now, as he twisted a hand in her hair to pull her head back. To plunder. No one had ever taken her like this. No one had ever warned her that a touch of violence could be so exciting. Her gasp of surprise turned into a moan of pleasure as his tongue skimmed over hers.

He thought of lightning bolts again, thought of that flash of power and light. She was electric in his arms, sparking, sizzling. Her scent, as soft, as seductive, as a whisper, clouded his mind, even as the taste of her heightened his appetite.

She was all woman, she was every woman, and yet she was like no other. He could hear each quick catch of her breath above the roar of the motor. With her name on his lips, he pressed them to the vulnerable line of her throat, where the skin was heated from the sun and as delicate as water.

She might have slid bonelessly to the deck if his body hadn't pressed hers so firmly against the rail. In wonder, in panic, she felt his muscles turn to iron wherever they touched her. Never before had she felt so fragile, so at the mercy of her own desires. The sea was as calm as glass, but she felt herself tossed, tumbled, wrecked. With a sigh that was almost a sob, she wrapped her arms around him.

It was the defenselessness of the gesture that pulled him back from the edge. He must have been mad. For a moment he'd been close, much too close, to dragging her down to the deck without a thought to her wishes or to the consequences. With his eyes closed, he held her, feeling the erratic beat of her heart, hearing her shallow, shuddering breath.

Perhaps he was still mad, Stephen thought. Even as the ragged edges of desire eased, something deeper and far more dangerous bloomed.

He wanted her, in a way no man could safely want a woman. Forever.

Fate, he thought again as he stroked her hair. It seemed he was falling in love whether he wished it or not. A few hours with her and he felt more than he had ever imagined he could feel.

There had been a few times in his life when he had seen and desired on instinct alone. What he had seen and desired, he had taken. Just as he would take her. But when he took, he meant to keep.

Carefully he stepped back. "Maybe neither of us has a choice." He dipped his hands into his pockets. "And if I touch you again, here, now, I won't give you one."

Unable to pretend, knowing they were shaking, she pushed her hands through her hair. She didn't bother to disguise the tremor in her voice. She wouldn't have known how. "I won't want one." She saw his eyes darken quickly, dangerously, but she didn't know his hands were balled into fists, straining.

"You make it difficult for me."

A long, shuddering breath escaped her. No one had ever wanted her this way. Probably no one ever would again. "I'm sorry. I don't mean to."

"No." Deliberately he relaxed his hands. "I don't think you do. That's one of the things about you I find most intriguing. I will have you, Rebecca." He saw something flicker in her eyes . . . Excitement? Panic? A combination of the two, perhaps. "Because I'm sure of it, because I know you're sure of it, I'll do my best to give you a little more time."

Her natural humor worked through the sliver of unease she felt. "I'm not sure whether I should thank you politely or run like hell."

He grinned, surprising himself, then flicked a finger down her cheek. "I wouldn't advise running, *matia mou*. I'd only catch you."

She was sure of that, too. One look at his face, even with the smile that softened it, and she knew. Kind, yes, but with a steely underlying ruthlessness. "Then I'll go with the thank-you."

"You're welcome." Patience, he realized, would have to be developed. And quickly. "Would you like to swim? There's a bay. We're nearly there."

The water might, just might, cool her off. "I'd love it."

Chapter Five

The water was cool and mirror-clear. Rebecca lowered herself into it with a sigh of pure pleasure. Back in Philadelphia she would have been at her desk, calculator clicking, the jacket of her neat business suit carefully smoothed over the back of her chair. Her figures would always tally, her forms would always be properly filed.

The dependable, efficient Miss Malone.

Instead, she was swimming in a crystal-clear bay, letting the water cool and the sun heat. Ledgers and accounts were worlds away. Here, as close as a hand-span, was a man who was teaching her everything she would ever want to know about needs, desires, and the fragility of the heart.

He couldn't know it, she thought. She doubted she'd ever have the courage to tell him that he was the only one who had ever made her tremble and burn. A man as physically aware as he would only be uncomfortable knowing he held an inexperienced woman in his arms.

The water lapped around her with a sound as quiet as her own sigh. But he didn't know, because when she was in his arms she didn't feel awkward and inexperienced. She felt beautiful, desirable and reckless.

With a laugh, Rebecca dipped under the surface to let the water, and the freedom, surround her. Who would have believed it?

"Does it always take so little to make you laugh?"

Rebecca ran a hand over her slicked-back hair. Stephen was treading water beside her, smoothly, hardly making a ripple. His skin was dark gold, glistening wet. His hair was streaked by the sun and dampened by the water, which was almost exactly the color of his eyes. She had to suppress an urge to just reach out and touch.

"A secluded inlet, a beautiful sky, an interesting man." With another sigh, she kicked her legs up so that she could float. "It doesn't seem like so little to me." She studied the vague outline of the mountains, far out of reach. "I promised myself that no matter where I went, what I did, I'd never take anything for granted again."

There was something in the way she said it, some hint of sadness, that pulled at him. The urge to comfort wasn't completely foreign in him, but he hadn't had much practice at it. "Was there a man who hurt you?"

Her lips curved at that, but he couldn't know that she was laughing at herself. Naturally, she'd dated. They had been polite, cautious evenings, usually with little interest on either side. She'd been dull, or at least she had never worked up the nerve to spread her wings. Once or twice, when she'd felt a tug, she'd been too shy, too much the efficient Rebecca Malone, to do anything about it.

With him, everything was different. Because she loved him. She didn't know how, she didn't know why, but she loved him as much as any woman could love any man.

"No. There's no one." She closed her eyes, trusting the water to carry her. "When my parents died, it hurt. It hurt so badly that I suppose I pulled back from life. I thought it was important that I be a responsible adult, even though I wasn't nearly an adult yet."

Strange that she hadn't thought of it quite that way until she'd stopped being obsessively responsible. Stranger still was how easy it was to tell him what she'd never even acknowledged herself.

"My aunt Jeannie was kind and considerate and loving, but she'd forgotten what it was like to be a young girl. Suddenly I realized I'd missed being young, lazy, foolish, all the things everyone's entitled to be at least once. I decided to make up for it."

Her hair was spread out and drifting on the water. Her eyes were closed, and her face was sheened with water. Not beautiful, Stephen told himself. She was too angular for real beauty. But she was fascinating . . . in looks, in philosophy . . . more, in the open-armed way she embraced whatever crossed her path.

He found himself looking around the inlet as he hadn't bothered to look at anything in years. He could see the sun dancing on the surface, could see the ripples spreading and growing from the quiet motion of their bodies. Farther away was the narrow curving strip of white beach, deserted now, but for a few birds fluttering over the sand. It was quiet, almost unnaturally quiet, the only sound the soft, monotonous slap of water against sand. And he was relaxed, totally, mind and body. Perhaps he, too, had forgotten what it was like to be young and foolish.

On impulse he put a hand on her shoulder and pushed her under.

She came up sputtering, dragging wet

hair out of her eyes. He grinned at her and calmly continued to tread water. "It was too easy."

She tilted her head, considering him and the distance between them. Challenge leaped into her eyes, sparked with amusement. "It won't be the next time."

His grin only widened. When he moved, he moved fast, streaking under and across the water like an eel. Rebecca had time for a quick squeal. Dragging in a deep breath, she kicked out. He caught her ankle, but she was ready. Unresisting, she let him pull her under. Then, instead of fighting her way back to the surface, she wrapped her arms around him and sent them both rolling in an underwater wrestling match. They were still tangled, her arms around him, her hands hooked over his shoulders, when they surfaced.

"We're even." She gasped for air and shook the water out of her eyes.

"How do you figure?"

"If we'd had a mat I'd have pinned you. Want to go for two out of three?"

"I might." He felt her legs tangle with his as she kicked out lazily. "But for now I prefer this."

He was going to kiss her again. She saw it in his eyes, felt it in the slight tensing of the arm that locked them torso to torso. She wasn't sure she was ready. More, she was afraid she was much too ready.

"Stephen?"

"Hmm?" His lips were a breath away from hers. Then he found himself underwater again, his arms empty. He should have been furious. He nearly was when he pushed to surface. She was shoulder-deep in the water, a few feet away. Her laughter rolled over him, young, delighted, unapologetic.

"It was too easy." She managed a startled "whoops" when he struck out after her. She might have made it — she had enough of a lead — but he swam as though he'd been born in the water. Still, she was agile, and she almost managed to dodge him, but her laughter betrayed her. She gulped in water, choked, then found herself hauled up into his arms in thigh-deep water.

"I like to win." Deciding it was useless to struggle, she pressed a hand to her heart and gasped for air. "It's a personality flaw. Sometimes I cheat at canasta."

"Canasta?" The last thing he could picture the slim, sexy bundle in his arms doing was spending a quiet evening playing cards.

"I can't help myself." Still breathless, she

laid her head on his shoulder. "No will-power."

"I find myself having the same problem." With a careless toss, he sent her flying through the air. She hit the water bottom first.

"I guess I deserved that." She struggled to her feet, water raining off her. "I have to sit." Wading through the water, she headed for the gentle slope of beach. She lay, half in and half out of the water, not caring that the sand would cling to her hair and skin. When he dropped down beside her, she reached out a hand for his. "I don't know when I've had a nicer day."

He looked down to where her fingers linked with his. The gesture had been so easy, so natural. He wondered how it could both comfort and arouse. "It's hardly over."

"It seems like it could last forever." She wanted it to go on and on. Blue skies and easy laughter. Cool water and endless hours. There had been a time, not so long before, when the days had dragged into nights and the nights into days. "Did you ever want to run away?"

With her hand still in his, he lay back to watch a few scattered rags of clouds drift. How long had it been, he wondered, since he'd really watched the sky? "To where?"

"Anywhere. Away from the way things are, away from what you're afraid they'll always be." She closed her eyes and could see herself brewing that first cup of coffee at exactly 7:15, opening the first file at precisely 9:01. "To drop out of sight," she murmured, "and pop up somewhere else, anywhere else, as someone completely different."

"You can't change who you are."

"Oh, but you can." Her tone suddenly urgent, she rose on her elbow. "Sometimes you have to."

He reached up to touch the ends of her hair. "What are you running from?"

"Everything. I'm a coward."

He looked into her eyes. They were so clear, so full of enthusiasm. "I don't think so."

"But you don't know me." A flicker of regret, then uncertainty, ran across her face. "I'm not sure I want you to."

"Don't I?" His fingers tightened on her hair, keeping her still. "There are people and circumstances that don't take months or years before they're understood. I look at you and something fits into place, Rebecca. I don't know why, but it is. I know you." He tugged her down for the

75

lightest, the briefest, of kisses. "And I like what I see."

"Do you?" She smiled. "Really?"

"Do you imagine I spend the day with a woman only because I want to sleep with her?" She shrugged, and though her blush was very faint, he noticed it and was amused by it. How many women, he wondered, could kiss a man into oblivion, then blush? "Being with you, Rebecca, is a difficult pleasure."

She chuckled and began to draw circles in the wet sand. What would he say, what would he think, if he knew what she was? Or, more accurately, what she wasn't? It didn't matter, she told herself. She couldn't let it spoil what there was between them.

"I think that's the most wonderful compliment I've ever had."

"Where have you been?" he murmured.

When she moved restlessly, he held her still. "Don't. I'm not going to touch you. Not yet."

"That's not the problem." With her eyes closed, she tilted her chin up and let the sun beat down on her face. "The problem is, I want you to touch me, so much it frightens me." Taking her time, she sat up, gathering her courage. She wanted to be honest, and she hoped she wouldn't sound like a fool. "Stephen, I don't sleep around. I need you to understand, because this is all happening so quickly. But it's not casual."

He lifted a hand to her chin and turned her to face him. His eyes were as blue as the water, and, to her, as unfathomable. "No, it's not." He made the decision quickly, though he had been turning the idea over in his mind all day. "I have to go to Athens tomorrow. Come with me, Rebecca."

"Athens?" she managed, staring at him.

"Business. A day, two at the most. I'd like you with me." And he was afraid, more than he cared to admit, that when he returned she might be gone.

"I . . ." What should she say? What was right?

"You told me you'd planned to go." He'd push if necessary. Now that the idea had taken root, Stephen had no intention of going anywhere without her.

"Yes, but I wouldn't want to be in the way while you're working."

"You'll be in my way whether you're here or there." Her head came up at that, and the look she gave him was both shy and stunning. He stifled the need to take her again, to roll until she was beneath him on the sand. He'd said he'd give her time. Perhaps what he'd really meant was that he needed time himself.

"You'll have your own suite. No strings, Rebecca. Just your company."

"A day or two," she murmured.

"It's a simple matter to have your room held for you here for your return."

Her return. Not his. If he left Corfu tomorrow she would probably never see him again. He was offering her another day, perhaps two. Never take anything for granted, she remembered. Never again.

Athens, she thought. It was true that she had planned to see it before she left Greece. But she would have gone alone. A few days before, that had been what she thought she wanted. The adventure of seeing new places, new people, on her own. Now the thought of going with him, of having him beside her when she first caught sight of the Acropolis, of having him want her with him, changed everything.

"I'd love to go with you." She rose quickly and dived into the water. She was in over her head.

Chapter Six

Athens was neither East nor West. It was spitted meat and spices roasting. It was tall buildings and modern shops. It was narrow, unpaved streets and clamorous bazaars. It had been the scene of revolution and brutality. It was ancient and civilized and passionate.

Rebecca quite simply fell in love at first sight.

She'd been seduced by Paris and charmed by London, but in Athens she lost her heart. She wanted to see everything at once, from sunrise to moonlight, and the heat-drenched afternoon between.

All that first morning, while Stephen was immersed in business meetings, she wandered. The hotel he'd chosen was lovely, but she was drawn to the streets and the people. Somehow she didn't feel like a visitor here. She felt like someone who had returned home after a long, long journey. Athens was waiting for her, ready to welcome her back.

Incredible. All her life she had accepted

the parameters set for her. Now she was touring Old Athens, with its clicking worry beads and its open-fronted shops, where she could buy cheap plaster copies of monuments or elegant antiques.

She passed tavernas, but she was too excited to be tempted by the rich smells of coffee and baking. She heard the clear notes of a flute as she looked up and saw the Acropolis.

There was only one approach. Though it was still early, other tourists were making their way toward the ruins in twos and in groups. Rebecca let her camera hang by its strap. Despite the chattering around her, she felt alone, but beautifully so.

She would never be able to explain what it felt like to stand in the morning sun and look at something that had been built for the gods — something that had endured war and weather and time. It had been a place of worship. Even now, after centuries had passed, Rebecca felt the spiritual pull. Perhaps the goddess Athena, with her gleaming helmet and spear, still visited there.

Rebecca had been disappointed that Stephen couldn't join her on her first morning in Athens. Now she was glad to be alone — to sit and absorb and imagine without having to explain her thoughts.

How could she, after having seen so much, go back to so little? Sighing, she wandered through the temples. It wasn't just the awe she felt here, or the excitement she had felt in London and Paris, that had changed her. It was Stephen and everything she'd felt, everything she'd wanted, since she'd met him.

Perhaps she would go back to Philadelphia, but she would never be the same person. Once you fell in love, completely, totally in love, nothing was ever the same.

She wished it could be simple, the way she imagined it was simple for so many other women. An attractive man, a physical tug. But with Stephen, as with Athens, she'd lost her heart. However implausible it seemed, she had recognized the man, as well as the city, as being part of her, as being for her. Desire, when tangled up with love, could never be simple.

But how could you be sure you were in love when it had never happened to you before? If she were home, at least she would have a friend to talk to. With a little laugh, Rebecca walked out into the sunlight. How many times had she been on the receiving end of a long, scattered conversation from a friend who had fallen in love — or thought she had. The excitement, the unhappiness, the thrills. Sometimes she'd been envious, and sometimes she'd been grateful not to have the complication in her own life. But always, always, she'd offered calm, practical, even soothing advice.

Oddly enough, she didn't seem to be able to do the same for herself.

All she could think of was the way her heart pounded when he touched her, how excitement, panic and anticipation fluttered through her every time he looked at her. When she was with him, her feelings and fantasies seemed reasonable. When she was with him, she could believe in fate, in the matching of soul to soul.

It wasn't enough. At least that was what she would have told another woman. Attraction and passion weren't enough. Yet there was no explaining, even to herself, the sense of rightness she experienced whenever she was with him. If she were a fanciful person she would say it was as though she'd been waiting for him, waiting for the time and the place for him to come to her.

It sounded simple — if fate could be considered simple. Yet beneath all the pleasure and that sense of reunion was guilt. She couldn't shake it, and she knew she wouldn't be able to ignore it much longer. She wasn't the woman she had let him believe her to be. She wasn't the well-traveled at-loose-ends free spirit she pretended to be. No matter how many ties she'd cut, she was still Rebecca Malone. How would he feel about her once he knew how limited and dull her life had been?

How and when was she going to tell him?

A few more days, she promised herself as she began the walk back. It was selfish, perhaps it was even dangerous, but she wanted just a few more days.

It was midafternoon before she returned to the hotel. Ignoring the fact that she might be considered overeager, she went straight to Stephen's suite. She couldn't wait to see him, to tell him everything she'd seen, to show him everything she'd bought. Her easy smile faded a bit when his secretary Elana opened the door.

"Miss Malone." Gracious and self-confident, Elana waved her in. "Please sit down. I'll let Stephen know you're here."

"I don't want to interrupt." Rebecca shifted her bags, feeling gauche and foolish.

"Not at all. Have you just come in?"

"Yes, I . . ." For the first time, Rebecca noticed that her skin was damp and her hair tousled. In contrast, Elana was cool and perfectly groomed. "I really should go."

"Please." Elana urged Rebecca to a chair. "Let me get you a drink." With a half smile, Elana began to pour a tall glass of iced juice. She had expected Stephen's mystery lady to be smooth, controlled and stunning. It pleased her a great deal to find Rebecca wide-eyed, a little unsure, and clearly a great deal in love.

"Did you enjoy your morning?"

"Yes, very much." She accepted the glass and tried to relax. Jealousy, she realized, feeling herself flush at the realization. She couldn't remember ever having experienced the sensation before. Who wouldn't be jealous? she asked herself as she watched Elana walk to the phone. The Greek woman was gorgeous, self-contained, coolly efficient. Above all, she had a relationship with Stephen that Rebecca knew nothing about. How long has she known him? Rebecca wondered. And how well?

"Stephen's just finishing up some business," Elana said as she hung up the phone. With easy, economical moves, she

84

poured herself a drink, then walked to the chair facing Rebecca. "What do you think of Athens?"

"I love it." Rebecca wished she'd taken the time to brush her hair and freshen her makeup. Lecturing herself, she sipped at her juice. "I'm not sure what I expected, but it's everything and more."

"Europeans see it as the East. Orientals see it as the West." Elana crossed her legs and settled back. It surprised her to realize that she was prepared to like Rebecca Malone. "What Athens is is Greek — and, more particularly, Athenian." She paused, studying Rebecca over the rim of her glass. "People often view Stephen in much the same way, and what he is is Stephen."

"How long have you worked for him?"

"Five years."

"You must know him well."

"Better than some. He's a demanding and generous employer and an interesting man. Fortunately, I like to travel and I enjoy my work."

Rebecca rubbed at a spot of dust on her slacks. "It never occurred to me that farming required so much traveling. I never realized how much was involved in growing olives."

Elana's brows rose in obvious surprise,

but she continued smoothly when Rebecca glanced back at her. "Whatever Stephen does, he does thoroughly." She smiled to herself, satisfied. She hadn't been certain until now whether the American woman was attracted to Stephen or to his position. "Has Stephen explained to you about the dinner party this evening?"

"He said something about a small party here at the hotel. A business dinner."

"Men take these things more lightly than women." Feeling friendlier, Elena offered her first genuine smile. "It will be small, but quite extravagant." She watched as Rebecca automatically lifted a hand to her hair. "If you need anything — a dress, a salon — the hotel can accommodate you."

Rebecca thought of the casual sportswear she'd tossed into her bag before the impulsive trip to Athens. "I need everything."

With a quick, understanding laugh, Elana rose. "I'll make some calls for you."

"Thank you, but I don't want to interfere with your work."

"Seeing that you're comfortable is part of my work." They both glanced over when the door opened. "Stephen. You see, she hasn't run away." Taking her glass and her pad, she left them alone.

"You were gone a long time." He hated the fact that he'd begun to watch the clock and worry. He'd imagined her hurt or abducted. He'd begun to wonder if she would disappear from his life as quickly as she'd appeared in it. Now she was here, her eyes alive with pleasure, her clothes rumpled and her hair windblown.

"I guess I got caught up exploring." She started to rise, but before she could gain her feet he was pulling her out of the chair, seeking, finding her mouth with his.

His desperation whipped through her. His hunger incited her own. Without thought, without hesitation, she clung to him, answering, accepting. Already seduced, she murmured something, an incoherent sound that caught in her throat.

Good God, he thought, it wasn't possible, it wasn't sane, to want like this. Throughout the morning while all the facts and figures and demands of business had been hammering at him, he'd thought of her, of holding her, of tasting her, of being with her. When she had stayed away for so long he'd begun to imagine, then to fear, what his life would be like without her.

It wasn't going to happen. He scraped his teeth over her bottom lip, and she

gasped and opened for him. He wouldn't
let it happen. Where she came from, where
she intended to go, no longer mattered.
She belonged to him now. And, though
he'd only begun to deal with it, he belonged to her.

But he needed some sanity, some logic.
Fighting himself, Stephen drew her away
from him. Her eyes remained closed, and
her lips remained parted. A soft, sultry
sound escaped them as her lashes fluttered
upward.

"I . . ." She took a deep breath and let it
out slowly. "I should go sightseeing more
often."

Gradually he realized how hard his fingers were pressing into her arms. As if he
were afraid she would slip away. Cursing
himself, he relaxed. "I would have preferred to go with you."

"I understand you're busy. I'd have
bored you silly, poking into every shop and
staring at every column."

"No." If there was one thing he was certain of, it was that she would never bore
him. "I'd like to have seen your first im-
pression of Athens."

"It was like coming home," she told him,
then hurried on because it sounded
foolish. "I couldn't get enough." Laughing

at herself, she gestured toward her bags. "Obviously. It's so different from anywhere I've ever been. At the Acropolis I couldn't even take any pictures, because I knew they couldn't capture the feeling. Then I walked along the streets and saw old men with *kom— konbou—*" She fumbled over the Greek and finally made a helpless gesture.

"*Komboulol,*" he murmured. "Worry beads."

"Yes, and I imagined how they might sit in those shadowy doorways watching the tourists go by, day after day, year after year." She sat, pleased to share her impressions with him. "I saw a shop with all these costumes, lots of tinsel, and some really dreadful plaster copies of the monuments."

He grinned and sat beside her. "How many did you buy?"

"Three or four." She bent down to rattle through her bags. "I bought you a present."

"A plaster statue of Athena?"

She glanced up, eyes laughing. "Almost. Then I found this tiny antique shop in the old section. It was all dim and dusty and irresistible. The owner had a handful of English phrases, and I had my phrase

book. After we'd confused each other completely, I bought this."

She drew out an S-shaped porcelain
pipe decorated with paintings of the wild
mountain goats of Greece. Attached to it
was a long wooden stem, as smooth as
glass, tipped by a tarnished brass mouth-
piece.

"I remembered the goats we'd seen on
Corfu," she explained as Stephen exam-
ined it. "I thought you might like it,
though I've never seen you smoke a pipe."

With a quiet laugh, he looked back at
her, balancing the gift in both hands.
"No, I don't — at least not of this na-
ture."

"Well, it's more ornamental than func-
tional, I suppose. The man couldn't tell
me much about it — at least not that I
could understand." She reached out to run
a finger along the edge of the bowl. "I've
never seen anything like it."

"I'm relieved to hear it." When she sent
him a puzzled look, he leaned over to
brush her lips with his. "*Matia mou,* this is
a hashish pipe."

"A hashish pipe?" She stared, first in
shock, then in fascination. "Really? I mean,
did people actually use it?"

"Undoubtedly. Quite a number, I'd say,

since it's at least a hundred and fifty years old."

"Imagine that." She pouted, imagining dark, smoky dens. "I guess it's not a very appropriate souvenir."

"On the contrary, whenever I see it I'll think of you."

She glanced up quickly, unsure, but the amusement in his eyes had her smiling again. "I should have bought you the plaster statue of Athena."

Taking her hands, he drew her to her feet. "I'm flattered that you bought me anything." She felt the subtle change as his fingers tightened on hers. "I want time with you, Rebecca. Hours of it. Days. There's too much I need to know." When she lowered her gaze, he caught her chin. "What are those secrets of yours?"

"Nothing that would interest you."

"You're wrong. Tomorrow I intend to find out all there is to know." He saw the quick flicker of unease in her eyes. Other men, he thought with an uncomfortable surge of jealousy. The hell with them. "No more evasions. I want you, all of you. Do you understand?"

"Yes, but —"

"Tomorrow." He cut her off, suddenly, completely, frustratingly Greek. "I have business that can't be avoided now. I'll come for you at seven."

"All right."

Tomorrow was years away, she told herself. She had time to decide what she would say, how she would say it. Before tomorrow came tonight. She would be everything she'd ever wanted to be, everything he wanted her to be.

"I'd better go." Before he could touch her again, she bent to gather her bags. "Stephen . . ." She paused at the door and turned to look at him as he stood in the middle of the room, comfortable with the wealth that surrounded him, confident with who and what he was. "You might be disappointed when you find out."

She left quickly, leaving him frowning after her.

Chapter Seven

She was as nervous as a cat. Every time she looked in the mirror Rebecca wondered who the woman was who was staring back at her. It wasn't a stranger, but it was a very, very different Rebecca Malone.

Was it just the different hairstyle, poufed and frizzed and swept around her face? Could it be the dress, the glittery spill of aquamarine that left her arms and shoulders bare? No, it was more than that. More than makeup and clever stylists and glamorous clothes. It was in her eyes. How could she help but see it? How could anyone? The woman who looked back from the mirror was a woman in love.

What was she going to do about it? What could she do? she asked herself. She was still practical enough to accept that some things could never be changed. But was she bold enough, or strong enough, to take what she wanted and live with the consequences?

When she heard the knock on the door,

Rebecca took a deep breath and picked up the useless compact-size evening bag she'd bought just that afternoon. It was all happening so fast. When she'd come back from Stephen's suite there had been a detailed message from Elana listing appointments — for a massage, a facial, hairstyling — along with the name of the manager of the hotel's most exclusive boutique. She hadn't had time to think, even for a minute, about her evening with Stephen. Or about any to-morrows.

Perhaps that was best, she decided as she pulled open the door. It was best not to think, not to analyze. It was best to accept and to act.

She looked like a siren, some disciple of Circe, with her windswept hair and a dress the color of seductive seas. Had he told himself she wasn't beautiful? Had he believed it? At that moment he was certain he'd never seen, never would see, a more exciting woman.

"You're amazing, Rebecca." He took her hand and drew her to him so that they stood in the doorway together. On the threshold.

"Why? Because I'm on time?"

"Because you're never what I expect."

He brought her hand to his lips. "And always what I want."

Because she was speechless, she was glad when he closed the door at her back and led her to the elevators. He looked different from the man she had first met, the one who dressed with such casual elegance. Tonight there was a formality about him, and the sophistication she had sensed earlier was abundantly apparent in the ease with which he wore the black dinner jacket.

"The way you look," he told her, "it seems a shame to waste the evening on a business dinner."

"I'm looking forward to meeting some of your friends."

"Associates," he said with an odd smile. "When you've been poor — and don't intend to be poor again — you rarely make friends in business."

She frowned. This was a side of him, the business side, that she didn't know. Would he be ruthless? She looked at him, saw it, and accepted it. Yes, a man like Stephen would always be ruthless with what belonged to him. "But enemies?"

"The same rule, in business, applies to friends and enemies. My father taught me more than fishing, Rebecca. He also taught me that to succeed, to attain, you must learn not only how to trust, but how far."

"I've never been poor, but I imagine it's frightening."

"Strengthening." He took her hand again when the elevator doors opened. "We have different backgrounds, Rebecca, but, fortunately, we've come to the same place."

He had no idea *how* different. Trust. He had spoken of trust. She discovered she wanted to tell him, tell him everything. Tell him that she knew nothing of elegant parties and glamorous life-styles. She was a fraud, and when he found out he might laugh at her and brush her aside. But she wanted him to know.

"Stephen, I want to —"

"Stephen. Once more you outdo us all in your choice of women."

"Dimitri."

Rebecca stopped, caught on the brink of confession. The man who faced her was classically handsome. His silver mane contrasted with bronzed skin lined by a half century of sun. He wore a mustache that swept majestically over gleaming teeth.

"It was kind of you to invite us here this evening, but it would be kinder still to introduce me to your lovely companion."

"Rebecca Malone, Dimitri Petropolis."

A diamond glittered on the hand he lifted to clasp Rebecca's. The hand itself was hard as rock. "A pleasure. Athens is already abuzz with talk of the woman who arrived with Stephen."

Certain he was joking, she smiled. "Then Athens must be in desperate need of news."

His eyes widened for a moment, then creased at the corners when he laughed. "I have no doubt you will provide an abundance of it."

Stephen slipped a hand under Rebecca's elbow. The look he sent Dimitri was very quick and very clear. They had competed over land, but there would be no competition over Rebecca.

"If you'll excuse us a moment, Dimitri, I'd like to get Rebecca some champagne."

"Of course." Amused — and challenged — Dimitri brushed at his mustache as he watched them walk away.

Rebecca had no way of knowing that to Stephen a small dinner party meant a hundred people. She sipped her first glass of wine, hoping she wouldn't embarrass them both by being foolishly shy and tongue-tied. In the past, whenever she had found herself in a crowd, she had always looked for the nearest corner to fade into. Not tonight, she promised herself, straightening her shoulders.

There were dozens of names to remember, but she filed them away as easily as she had always filed numbers. In the hour before dinner, while the guests mixed and mingled, she found herself at ease. The stomach flutters and hot blushes she'd often experienced at parties and functions simply didn't happen.

Perhaps she was the new Rebecca Malone after all.

She heard business discussed here and there. Most of it seemed to be hotel and resort business — talk of remodeling and expansions, mergers and takeovers. She found it odd that so many of the guests were in that trade, rather than prosperous farmers or olive growers.

Stephen came up behind her and murmured in her ear, "You look pleased with yourself."

"I am." He couldn't know that she was pleased to find herself at ease and comfortable in a party of strangers. "So many interesting people."

"Interesting." He brushed a finger over

her wispy bangs. "I thought you might find it dull."

"Not at all." She took a last sip of champagne, then set the glass aside. Instantly a waiter was at her side, offering another. Stephen watched her smile her thanks.

"So you enjoy parties?"

"Sometimes. I'm enjoying this one, and having a chance to meet your associates."

Stephen glanced over her shoulder, summing up the looks and quiet murmurs. "They'll be talking about you for weeks to come."

She only laughed, turning in a slow circle. Around her was the flash of jewels and the gleam of gold. The sleek and the prosperous, the rich and the successful. It pleased her that she'd found more to talk about than tax shelters.

"I can't imagine they have so little on their minds. This is such a gorgeous room."

She looked around the huge ballroom, with its cream-and-rose walls, its glittering chandeliers and its gleaming floors. There were alcoves for cozy love seats and tall, thriving ornamental trees in huge copper pots. The tables, arranged to give a sense of intimacy, were already set with ivory cloths and slender tapers.

"It's really a beautiful hotel," she continued. "Everything about it runs so smoothly." She smiled up at him. "I'm torn between the resort in Corfu and this."

"Thank you." When she gave him a blank look, he tipped up her chin with his finger. "They're mine."

"Your what?"

"My hotels," he said simply, then led her to a table.

She spoke all through dinner, though for the first fifteen minutes she had no idea what she said. There were eight at Stephen's table, including Dimitri, who had shifted name cards so that he could sit beside her. She toyed with her seafood appetizer, chatted and wondered if she could have made a bigger fool out of herself.

He wasn't simply prosperous. He wasn't simply well-off. There was enough accountant left in Rebecca to understand that when a man owned what Stephen owned he was far, far more than comfortable.

What would he think of her when he found out what she was? Trust? How could she ever expect him to trust her now? She swallowed without tasting and managed to smile. Would he think she was a gold digger, that she had set herself up to run into him?

No, that was ridiculous.

She forced herself to look over and saw that Stephen was watching her steadily. She picked up her fork with one hand and balled up the napkin in her lap with the other.

Why couldn't he be ordinary? she wondered. Someone vacationing, someone working at the resort? Why had she fallen in love with someone so far out of her reach?

"Have you left us?"

Rebecca jerked herself back to see Dimitri smiling at her. Flushing, she noticed that the next course had been served while she'd been daydreaming. "I'm sorry." With an effort she began to toy with the *salata Athenas.*

"A beautiful woman need never apologize for being lost in her own thoughts." He patted her hand, then let his fingers linger. He caught Stephen's dark look and smiled. If he didn't like the boy so much, he thought, he wouldn't get nearly so much pleasure from irritating him. "Tell me, how did you meet Stephen?"

"We met in Corfu." She thought of that first meal they had shared . . . quiet, relaxed, alone.

"Ah, soft nights and sunny days. You are vacationing?"

"Yes." Rebecca put more effort into her smile. If she stared into her salad she would only embarrass herself, and Stephen. "He was kind enough to show me some of the island."

"He knows it well, and many of the other islands of our country. There's something of the gypsy in him."

She had sensed that. Hadn't that been part of the attraction? Hadn't Rebecca just discovered the gypsy in herself? "Have you known him long?"

"We have a long-standing business relationship. Friendly rivals, you might say. When Stephen was hardly more than a boy he accumulated an impressive amount of land." He gestured expansively. "As you can see, he used it wisely. I believe he has two hotels in your country."

"Two? More?" Rebecca picked up her glass and took a long swallow of wine.

"So you see, I had wondered if you had met in America and were old friends."

"No." Rebecca nodded weakly as the waiter removed the salad and replaced it with moussaka. "We only just met a few days ago."

"As always, Stephen moves quickly and stylishly." Dimitri took her hand again, more than a little amused by the frown he saw deepening in Stephen's eyes. "Where is it in America you are from?"

"Philadelphia." Relax, she ordered herself. Relax and enjoy. "That's in the Northeast."

It infuriated Stephen to watch her flirting so easily, so effectively, with another man. She sat through course after course, barely eating, all the while gifting Dimitri with her shy smiles. Not once did she draw away when the older man touched her hand or leaned close. From where he sat, Stephen could catch a trace of her scent, soft, subtle, maddening. He could hear her quiet laugh when Dimitri murmured something in her ear.

Then she was standing with him, her hand caught in his, as he led her to the dance floor.

Stephen sat there, battling back a jealousy he despised, and watched them move together to music made for lovers. Under the lights her dress clung, then swayed, then shifted. Her face was close, too damn close, to Dimitri's. He knew what it was like to hold her like that, to breathe in the scent of her skin and her hair. He knew what it was to feel her body brush against his, to feel the life, the passion, bubbling. He knew what it was to see her eyes blur, her lips part, to hear that quiet sigh.

He had often put his stamp on land, but never on a woman. He didn't believe in it. But only a fool sat idly by and allowed another man to enjoy what was his. With a muttered oath, Stephen rose, strode out onto the dance floor and laid a hand on Dimitri's shoulder.

"Ah, well." The older man gave a regretful sigh and stepped aside. "Until later."

Before she could respond, Rebecca was caught against Stephen. With a sigh of her own, she relaxed and matched her steps to his. Maybe it was like a dream, she told herself as she closed her eyes and let the music fill her head. But she was going to enjoy every moment until it was time to wake up.

She seemed to melt against him. Her fingers moved lightly through his hair as she rested her cheek against his. Was this the way she'd danced with Dimitri? Stephen wondered, then cursed himself. He was being a fool, but he couldn't seem to stop himself. Then again, he'd had to fight for everything else in his life. Why should his woman be any different?

He wanted to drag her off then and

there, away from everyone, and find some dark, quiet place to love her.

"You're enjoying yourself?"

"Yes." She wouldn't think about what he was, not now. Soon enough the night would be over and tomorrow would have to be faced. While the music played and he held her, she would only think of what he meant to her. "Very much."

The dreamy tone of her voice almost undid him. "Apparently Dimitri entertained you well."

"Mmm. He's a very nice man."

"You moved easily from his arms to mine."

Something in his tone pried through the pleasure she felt. Carefully she drew back so that she could see his face. "I don't think I know what you mean."

"I believe you do."

She was tempted to laugh, but there was no humor in Stephen's eyes. Rebecca felt her stomach knot as it always did when she was faced with a confrontation. "If I do, then I'd have to think you ridiculous. Maybe we'd better go back to the table."

"So you can be with him?" Even as the words came out he realized the unfairness, even the foolishness, of them.

She stiffened, retreating as far as she

could from anger. "I don't think this is the place for this kind of discussion."

"You're quite right." As furious with himself as he was with her, he pulled her from the dance floor.

Chapter Eight

"Stop it." By the time he'd dragged her to the elevators, Rebecca had gotten over her first shock. "What's gotten into you?"

"I'm simply taking you to a more suitable place for our discussion." He pulled her into the elevator, then punched the button for their floor.

"You have guests," she began, but he sent her a look that made her feel like a fool. Falling back on dignity, she straightened her shoulders. "I prefer to be asked if I want to leave, not dragged around as though I were a pack mule."

Though her heart was pounding, she sailed past him when the doors opened, intending to breeze into her own rooms and slam the door in his face. In two steps he had her arm again. Rebecca found herself guided, none too gently, into Stephen's suite.

"I don't want to talk to you," she said, because she was certain her teeth would begin to chatter at any moment. She didn't argue well in the best of circumstances.

Faced with Stephen's anger, she was certain she would lose.

He said nothing as he loosened his tie and the first two buttons of his shirt. He went to the bar and poured two brandies. He was being irrational and he knew it, but he seemed unable to control it. That was new, he decided. But there had been many new emotions in him since Rebecca.

Walking back to Rebecca, he set one snifter by her elbow. When he looked at her . . . he wanted to shout, to beg, to demand, to plead. As a result, his voice was clipped and hard.

"You came to Athens with me, not with Dimitri or any other man."

She didn't touch the snifter. She was certain her hands would shake so hard that it would slip out of her grip. "Is that a Greek custom?" It amazed her — and bolstered her confidence — to hear how calm her voice was. "Forbidding a woman to speak to another man?"

"Speak?" He could still see the way Dimitri had bent his head close to hers. Dimitri, who was smooth and practiced. Dimitri, whose background would very likely mirror Rebecca's. Old money, privileged childhoods, quiet society. "Do you allow every man who speaks to you to hold you, to touch you?"

She didn't blush. Instead, the color faded from her cheeks. She shook, not with fear but with fury. "What I do, and with whom I do it, is my business. Mine."

Very deliberately he lifted his snifter and drank. "No."

"If you think that because I came here with you you have the right to dictate to me you're wrong. I'm my own person, Stephen." It struck her even as she said it that it was true. She was her own person. Each decision she made was her own. Filled with a new sense of power, she stepped forward. "No one owns me, not you, not anyone. I won't be ordered. I won't be forced. I won't be pressured." With a flick of her skirts, she turned. He had her again quickly, his hands on both of her arms, his face close.

"You won't go back to him."

"You couldn't stop me if that was what I wanted." She tossed her head back challengingly. "But I have no intention of going back downstairs to Dimitri, or anyone else." She jerked her arms free. "You idiot. Why should I want to be with him when I'm in love with you?"

She stopped, her eyes wide with shock,

her lips parted in surprise. Overwhelmed by a combination of humiliation and fury, she spun around. Then she was struggling against him. "Leave me alone! Oh, God, just leave me alone!"

"Do you think I could let you go now?" He caught her hair in his hand, dragging it back until her eyes met his. In them she saw triumph and desire. "I feel as though I've waited all my life to hear you say those words." He rained kisses over her face until her struggles ceased. "You drive me mad," he murmured. "Being with you, being without you."

"Please." Colors, shapes, lights were whirling in her head. "I need to think."

"No. Ask me for anything else, but not more time." Gathering her close, he buried his face in her hair. "Do you think I make a fool of myself over every woman?"

"I don't know." She moaned when his lips trailed down her throat. Something wild and terrifying was happening inside her body. "I don't know you. You don't know me."

"Yes, I do." He pulled away just far enough to look down at her. "From the first moment I saw you, I knew you. Needed you. Wanted you."

It was true. She knew it, felt it, but she

shook her head in denial. "It's not possible."

"I've loved you before, Rebecca, almost as much as I do now." He felt her go still. The color fled from her face again, but her eyes stayed steady on his.

"I don't want you to say what isn't real, what you're not sure of."

"Didn't you feel it, the first time I kissed you?" When he saw the acknowledgment in her eyes, his grip tightened. He could feel her heart thundering, racing to match the rhythm of his own. "Somehow you've come back to me, and I to you. No more questions," he said, before she could speak. "I need you tonight."

It was real. She felt the truth and the knowledge when his mouth found hers. If it was wrong to go blindly into need, then she would pay whatever price was asked. She could no longer deny him . . . or herself.

There was no gentleness in the embrace. It was as it had been the first time, lovers reunited, a hunger finally quenched. All heat and light. She gave more than she'd known she had. Her mouth was as avid as his, as seeking. Her murmurs were as desperate. Her hands didn't shake as they moved over him. They pressed, gripped,

111

demanded. Greedy, she tugged the jacket from his shoulders.

Yes, he'd come back to her. If it was madness to believe it, then for tonight she'd be mad.

The taste of her, just the taste of her, was making his head swim and his blood boil. He nipped at her lip, then sucked until he heard her helpless whimper. He wanted her helpless. Something fierce and uncivilized inside him wanted her weak and pliant and defenseless. When she went limp in his arms he dived into her mouth and plundered. Her response tore at him, so sweet, so vulnerable, then suddenly so ardent.

Her hands, which had fluttered helplessly to her side, rose up again to pull at his shirt, to race under it to warmed flesh. She could only think of how right it felt to touch him, to press against him and wait for him to light new fires inside her.

With an oath, he swept her up into his arms and carried her to the bedroom.

The moon was waning and offered only the most delicate light. It fell in slants and shadows on the bed, dreamlike. But the vibrating of Rebecca's pulse told her this was no dream. There was the scent of jasmine from the sprigs in the vase beside the bed.

It was a scent she would always remember, just as she would remember how dark and deep were the color of his eyes.

Needful, desperate, they tumbled onto the bed.

He wanted to take care with her. She seemed so small, so fragile. He wanted to show her how completely she filled his heart. But his body was on fire, and she was already moving like a whirlwind beneath him.

His mouth was everywhere, making her shudder and arch and ache. Desires she'd never known sprang to life inside her and took control. Delirious, she obeyed them, reveled in them, then searched for more.

They rolled across the bed in a passionate war that would have two victors, touching, taking, discovering. Impatient, he peeled the dress from her, moaning as he found her breasts with his hands, his lips, his teeth. Unreasoning desire catapulted through him when he felt her soar.

Her body felt like a furnace, impossibly hot, impossibly strong. Sensations rammed into her, stealing her breath. Mindless and moaning, she writhed under him, open for any demand he might make, pulsing for any new knowledge he might offer.

Finally, finally, she knew what it was to

love, to be loved, to be wanted beyond reason. Naked, she clung to him, awash in the power and the weakness, the glory and the terror.

He raced over her as if he already knew what would make her tremble, what would make her yearn. Never before had she been so aware, so in tune with another.

She made him feel like a god. He touched, and her skin vibrated under his hand. He tasted, and her flavor was like no other. She was moist, heated, and utterly willing. She seemed to explode beneath him, lost in pleasure, drugged by passion. No other woman had ever driven him so close to madness. Her head was thrown back, and one hand was flung out as her fingers dug into the sheets. Wanton, waiting, wild.

With her name on his lips, he drove into her. His breath caught. His mind spun. Her cry of pain and release echoed in his head, bringing him both triumph and guilt. His body went rigid as he fought to claw his way back. Then she seemed to close around him, body, heart, soul. As helpless as she, he crossed the line into madness and took her with him.

Chapter Nine

Aftershocks of passion wracked her. Stunned and confused, she lay in the shadowed light. Nothing had prepared her for this. No one had ever warned her that pleasure could be so huge or that need could be so jagged. If she had known . . . Rebecca closed her eyes and nearly laughed out loud. If she had known, she would have left everything behind years ago and searched the world for him.

Only him. She let out a quiet, calming sigh. Only him.

He was cursing himself, slowly, steadily, viciously. Innocent. Dear God. She'd been innocent, as fresh and untouched as spring, and he'd used her, hurt her, taken her.

Disgusted with himself, he sat up and reached for a cigar. He needed more than tobacco. He needed a drink, but he didn't trust his legs to carry him.

The flick of his lighter sounded like a gunshot. For an instant his face, hardened by anger and self-loathing, was illuminated.

"Why didn't you tell me?"

Still floating on an ocean of pleasure, she blinked her eyes open. "What?"

"Damn it, Rebecca, why didn't you tell me you hadn't been with a man before? That this — that I was your first?"

There was an edge of accusation in his voice. For the first time, she realized she was naked. Her cheeks grew hot as she fumbled for the sheet. One moment there was glory; the next, shame. "I didn't think of it."

"Didn't think of it?" His head whipped around. "Don't you think I had a right to know? Do you think this would have happened if I had known?"

She shook her head. It was true that she hadn't thought of it. It hadn't mattered. He was the first, the last, the only. But now it occurred to her that a man like him might not want to make love with an inexperienced woman. "I'm sorry." Her heart seemed to shrivel in her breast. "You said that you loved me, that you wanted me. The rest didn't seem to matter."

She'd cried out. He'd heard the shock and pain in her voice. And he hadn't been able to stop himself. Yes, he needed a drink. "It mattered," he tossed back as he rose and strode into the other room.

Alone, she let out a shuddering breath. Of course it mattered. Only a fool would have thought otherwise. He'd thought he was dealing with an experienced, emotionally mature woman who knew how to play the game. Words like *love* and *need* and *want* were interchangeable. Yes, he'd said he loved her, but to many love was physical and physical only.

She'd made a fool of herself and she'd infuriated him, and all because she'd begun a relationship built on illusions.

She'd knowingly taken the risk, Rebecca reminded herself as she climbed out of bed. Now she'd pay the price.

He was calmer when he started back to the bedroom. Calmer, though anger still bubbled inside him. First he would show her how it should have been, how it could be. Then they had to talk, rationally, coherently.

"Rebecca . . ." But when he looked at the bed it was empty.

She was wrapped in a robe and was hurling clothing into her suitcase when she heard him knock. With a shake of her head, she rubbed the tears from her cheeks and continued her frenzied packing. She wouldn't answer. . . . She wouldn't answer and be humiliated again.

"Rebecca." The moment of calm he'd achieved had vanished. Swearing through gritted teeth, he pounded on the door. "Rebecca, this is ridiculous. Open this door."

Ignoring him, she swept bottles and tubes of toiletries off the bureau and into her bag. He'd go away, she told herself, hardly aware that she'd begun to sob. He'd go away and then she'd leave, take a cab to the airport and catch the first plane to any-where.

The sound of splintering wood had her rushing into the parlor in time to see the door give way.

She'd thought she'd seen fury before, but she'd been wrong. She saw it now as she stared into Stephen's face. Speechless, she looked from him to the broken door and back again.

Elana, tying the belt of her robe, rushed down the hall. "Stephen, what's happened? Is there a —"

He turned on her, hurling one short sentence in clipped Greek at her. Her eyes widened and she backed away, sending Rebecca a look that combined sympathy and envy.

"Do you think you have only to walk away from me?" He pushed the door back until it scraped against the battered jamb.

"I want —" Rebecca lifted a hand to her throat as if to push the words out. "I want to be alone."

"The hell with what you want." He started toward her, only to stop dead when she cringed and turned away. He'd forgotten what it was like to hurt, truly hurt, until that moment. "I asked you once if you were afraid of me. Now I see that you are." Searching for control, he dipped his hands into the pockets of the slacks he'd thrown on. She looked defenseless, terrified, and tears still streaked her cheeks. "I won't hurt you again. Will you sit?" When she shook her head, he bit off an oath. "I will."

"I know you're angry with me," she began when he'd settled into a chair. "I'll apologize if it'll do any good, but I do want to be alone."

His eyes had narrowed and focused. "You'll apologize? For what?"

"For . . ." What did he expect her to say? Humiliated, she crossed her arms and hugged her elbows. "For what happened . . . for not . . . explaining," she finished lamely. "For whatever you like," she continued as the tears started again. "Just leave me alone."

"Sweet God." He rubbed a weary hand over his face. "I can think of nothing in my life I've handled as badly as this." He rose, but stopped again when she automatically retreated. "You don't want me to touch you." His voice had roughened. He had to swallow to clear his throat. "I won't, but I hope you'll listen."

"There's nothing more to say. I understand how you feel and why you feel it. I'd rather we just left it at that."

"I treated you inexcusably."

"I don't want an apology."

"Rebecca —"

"I don't." Her voice rose, stopping his words, stopping her tears. "It's my fault. It's been my fault all along. No, no, no!" she shouted when he took another step. "I don't want you to touch me. I couldn't bear it."

He sucked in his breath, then let it out slowly. "You twist the knife well."

But she was shaking her head and pacing the room now. "It didn't matter at first — at least I didn't think it would matter. I didn't know who you were or that I would fall in love with you. Now I've waited too long and ruined everything."

"What are you talking about?"

Perhaps it was best, best for both of

them, to lay out the truth. "You said you knew me, but you don't, because I've done nothing but lie to you, right from the first moment."

Slowly, carefully, he lowered himself to the arm of a chair. "What have you lied to me about?"

"Everything." Her eyes were drenched with regret when she looked at him. "Then, tonight . . . First I found out that you own hotels. *Own* them."

"It was hardly a secret. Why should it matter?"

"It wouldn't." She dropped her hands to her sides. "If I was what I'd pretended to be. After we'd made love and you — I realized that by pretending I'd let you have feelings for someone who didn't even exist."

"You're standing in front of me, Rebecca. You exist."

"No. Not the way you think, not the way I've let you think."

He prepared himself for the worst. "What have you done? Were you running away from America?"

"No. Yes." She had to laugh at that. "Yes, I was running." She gathered what composure she had left and folded her hands. "I did come from Philadelphia, as I told you. I've lived there all my life. Lived there, went to school there, worked there." She found a tissue in the pocket of her robe. "I'm an accountant."

He stared at her, one brow lifting, as she blew her nose. "I beg your pardon?"

"I said, I'm an accountant." She hurled the words at him, then whirled away to face the window. Stephen started to rise, then thought better of it.

"I find it difficult to imagine you tallying ledgers, Rebecca. If you'd sit down, maybe we could talk this through."

"Damn it, I said I'm an accountant. A CPA, specializing in corporate taxes. Up until a few weeks ago I worked for McDowell, Jableki and Kline in Philadelphia."

He spread his hands, taking it all in. "All right. What did you do? Embezzle?"

She tossed back her head and nearly exploded with laughter. If she said yes he'd probably be intrigued. But the time for intrigue was over. The time for the truth was now. "No. I've never done anything illegal in my life. I've never even had a parking ticket. I've never done anything at all out of the ordinary until a few weeks ago."

She began to pace again, too agitated to keep still. "I'd never traveled, never had a man send a bottle of champagne to my table, never walked along the beach in the moonlight, never had a lover."

He said nothing, not because he was angry or bored but because he was fascinated.

"I had a good job, my car was paid for, I had good, conservative investments that would have ensured me a comfortable retirement. In my circle of friends I'm known as dependable. If someone needs a sitter they know they can call Rebecca. If they need advice or someone to feed their fish while they're on vacation they don't have to worry. I was never late for work, never took five minutes extra for lunch."

"Commendable," he said, and earned a glare.

"Just the type of employee I imagine you'd like to hire."

He swallowed a chuckle. He'd been prepared for her to confess she had a husband, five husbands, a prison record. Instead she was telling him she was an accountant with an excellent work record. "I have no desire to hire you, Rebecca."

"Just as well." She turned away and started to prowl the room again. "You'd undoubtedly change your mind after I tell you the rest."

Stephen crossed his ankles and settled back. God, what a woman she was. "I'm anxious to hear it."

"My aunt died about three months ago, suddenly."

"I'm sorry." He would have gone to her then, but he could see she was far from ready. "I know how difficult it is to lose family."

"She was all I had left." Because she needed something to do, she pushed open the balcony doors. Warm, fragrant night air rushed in. "I couldn't believe she was gone. Just like that. No warning. Of course, I handled the funeral arrangements. No fuss, no frills. Just the way Aunt Jeannie would have wanted. She was a very economical woman, not only in finances but in dress, in speech, in manner. As long as I can remember, people compared me to her."

Stephen's brow lifted again as he studied the woman being buffeted by the breeze — the short red silk robe, the tousled hair.

"Soon after her death — I don't know if it was days or a week — something just snapped. I looked at myself, at my life, and I hated it." She dragged her hair back, only to have the wind catch it again. "I was a good employee, just like my aunt, a good credit risk, a dependable friend. Law-abiding, conservative and boring. Suddenly I could see myself ten, twenty, thirty years down the road, with nothing more than I had at that moment. I couldn't stand it."

She turned around. The breeze caught at the hem of her robe and sent it dancing around her legs. "I quit my job, and I sold everything."

"Sold?"

"Everything I owned — car, apartment, furniture, books, absolutely everything. I turned all the cash into traveler's checks, even the small inheritance from my aunt. Thousands of dollars. I know it might not sound like a lot to you, but it was more than I'd ever imagined having at once."

"Wait." He held up a hand, wanting to be certain he understood everything. "You're telling me that you sold your possessions, *all* your possessions?"

She couldn't remember ever having felt more foolish, and she straightened her shoulders defensively. "Right down to my coffeepot."

"Amazing," he murmured.

"I bought new clothes, new luggage, and flew to London. First-class. I'd never been on a plane before in my life."

"You'd never flown, but took your first trip across the Atlantic."

She didn't hear the admiration in his voice, only the amusement. "I wanted to see something different. To *be* something different. I stayed at the Ritz and took pictures of the changing of the guard. I flew to Paris and had my hair cut." Self-consciously she lifted a hand to it.

Because he could see that she was over-wrought, he was careful not to smile. "You flew to Paris for a haircut."

"I'd heard some women discussing this stylist, and I — Never mind." It was no use trying to explain that she'd gone to the same hairdresser, to the same shops, for years. The same everything. "Right after Paris, I came here," she went on. "I met you. Things happened. I let them happen." Tears threatened. She could only pray he didn't see them. "You were exciting, and attracted to me. Or attracted to who you thought I was. I'd never had a romance. No one had ever looked at me the way you did."

Once more he chose his words carefully. "Are you saying that being with me was different? An adventure, like flying to a Paris salon?"

She would never be able to explain what

being with him had meant to her. "Apologies and explanations really don't make any difference now. But I am sorry, Stephen. I'm sorry for everything."

He didn't see the tears, but he heard the regret in her voice. His eyes narrowed. His muscles tensed. "Are you apologizing for making love with me, Rebecca?"

"I'm apologizing for whatever you like. I'd make it up to you if I could, but I don't know how, unless I jump out the window."

He paused, as if he were considering it. "I don't think this requires anything quite that drastic. Perhaps if you'd sit down calmly?"

She shook her head and stayed where she was. "I can't handle any more of this tonight, Stephen. I'm sorry. You've every right to be angry."

He rose, the familiar impatience building. But she was so pale, looked so fragile, sounded so weary. He hadn't treated her gently before. At least he could do so now.

"All right. Tomorrow, then, after you've rested." He started to go to her, then checked himself. It would take time to show her that there were other ways to love. Time to convince her that love was more, much more than an adventure. "I want you to know that I regret what happened tonight. But that, too, will wait until tomorrow." Though he wanted to touch a hand to her cheek, he kept it fisted in his pocket. "Get some rest."

She had thought her heart was already broken. Now it shattered. Not trusting her voice, she nodded.

He left her alone. The door scraped against the splintered jamb as he secured it. She supposed there might have been a woman somewhere who'd made a bigger fool of herself. At the moment, it didn't seem to matter.

At least there was something she could do for both of them. Disappear.

Chapter Ten

It was her own fault, she supposed. There were at least half a dozen promising accounting positions in the want ads. Not one of them interested her. Rebecca circled them moodily. How could she be interested in dental plans and profit sharing? All she could think about, all she'd been able to think about for two weeks, was Stephen.

What had he thought when he'd found her gone? Relief? Perhaps a vague annoyance at business left unfinished? Pen in hand, Rebecca stared out of the window of the garden apartment she'd rented. In her fantasies she imagined him searching furiously for her, determined to find her, whatever the cost. Reality, she thought with a sigh, wasn't quite so romantic. He would have been relieved. Perhaps she wasn't sophisticated, but at least she'd stepped out of his life with no fuss.

Now it was time to get her own life in order.

First things first. She had an apartment, and the little square of lawn outside the glass doors was going to make her happy. That in itself was a challenge. Her old condo had been centrally located on the fifth floor of a fully maintained modern building.

This charming and older development was a good thirty miles from downtown, but she could hear the birds in the morning. She would be able to look out at old oaks and sweeping maples and flowers she would plant herself. Perhaps it wasn't as big a change as a flight to Paris, but for Rebecca it was a statement.

She'd bought some furniture. *Some* was the operative word. Thus far she'd picked out a bed, one antique table and a single chair.

Not logical, Rebecca thought with a faint smile. No proper and economical living room suite, no tidy curtains. Even the single set of towels she'd bought was frivolous. And exactly what she'd wanted. She would do what she'd secretly wanted to do for years — buy a piece here, a piece there. Not because it was a good buy or durable, but because she wanted it.

She wondered how many people would really understand the satisfaction of making decisions not because they were sensible but because they were desirable.

She'd done it with her home, her wardrobe. Even with her hair, she thought, running a hand through it. Outward changes had led to inner changes. Or vice versa. Either way, she would never again be the woman she'd been before.

Or perhaps she would be the woman she'd always been but had refused to acknowledge.

Then why was she circling ads in the classifieds? Rebecca asked herself. Why was she sitting here on a beautiful morning planning a future she had no interest in? Perhaps it was true that she would never have the one thing, the one person, she really wanted. There would be no more picnics or walks in the moonlight or frantic nights in bed. Still, she had the memories, she had the moments, she had the dreams. There would be no regrets where Stephen was concerned. Not now, and not ever. And if she was now more the woman she had been with him, it had taken more than a change in hairstyle.

She was stronger. She was surer. She was freer. And she'd done it herself.

She could think of nothing she wanted less than to go back into someone else's firm, tallying figures, calculating profit and loss. So she wouldn't. Rebecca sank into the chair as the thought struck home.

She wouldn't. She wouldn't go job hunting, carrying her résumé, rinsing sweaty palms in the rest room, putting her career and life in someone else's hands again. She'd open her own firm. A small one, certainly. Personalized. Exclusive, she decided, savoring the word. Why not? She had the skill, the experience, and — finally — she had the courage.

It wouldn't be easy. In fact, it would be risky. The money she had left would have to go toward renting office space, equipment, a phone system, advertising. With a bubbling laugh, she sprang up and searched for a legal pad and a pencil. She had to make lists — not only of things to do but of people to call. She had enough contacts from her McDowell, Jableki and Kline days. Maybe, just maybe, she could persuade some of her former clients to give her a try.

"Just a minute," she called out when she heard the knock on the door. She scribbled a reminder to look for file cabinets as she went to answer. She'd much rather have some good solid oak file cabinets than a living room sofa.

She knew better than to open the door without checking the security peephole, but she was much too involved with her plans to think about such things. When she opened the door, she found herself face-to-face with Stephen.

Even if she could have spoken, he wasn't in the mood to let her. "What in the hell do you think you're doing?" he demanded as he slammed the door behind him. "Do you deliberately try to drive me mad, or does it come naturally to you?"

"I — I don't —" But he was already yanking her against him. Whatever words she might have spoken dissolved into a moan against his lips. Her pad fell to the floor with a slap. Even as her arms came up around him he was thrusting her away.

"What kind of game are you playing, Rebecca?" When she just shook her head, he dug his hands into his pockets and paced the wide, nearly empty room. He was unshaven, disheveled and absolutely gorgeous. "It's taken me two weeks and a great deal of trouble to find you. I believe we'd agreed to talk again. I was surprised to discover you'd not only left Athens, but Europe." He swung back and pinned her with a look. "Why?"

Still reeling from his entrance, she struggled not to babble. "I thought it best that I leave."

"You thought?" He took a step toward her, his fury so palatable that she braced herself. "You thought it best," he repeated. "For whom?"

"For you. For both of us." She caught herself fiddling with the lapels of her robe and dropped her hands. "I knew you were angry with me for lying to you and that you regretted what had happened between us. I felt it would be better for both of us if I —"

"Ran away?"

Her chin came up fractionally. "Went away."

"You said you loved me."

She swallowed. "I know."

"Was that another lie?"

"Please don't." She turned away, but there was nowhere to go. "Stephen, I never expected to see you again. I'm trying to make some sense out of my life, to do things in a way that's not only right but makes me happy. In Greece, I guess, I did what made me happy, but I didn't think about what was right. The time with you was . . ."

"Was what?"

Dragging both hands through her hair, she turned to him again. It was as if the two weeks had never been. She was facing him again, trying to explain what she feared she could never explain. "It was the best thing that ever happened to me, the most important, the most unforgettable, the most precious. I'll always be grateful for those few days."

"Grateful." He wasn't sure whether to laugh or murder her. Stepping forward, he surprised them both by slipping his hands lightly around her throat. "For what? For my giving you your first fling? A fast, anonymous romance with no consequences?"

"No." She lifted a hand to his wrist but made no attempt to struggle. "Did you come all this way to make me feel more guilty?"

"I came all this way because I finish what I begin. We'd far from finished, Rebecca."

"All right." Be calm, she told herself. When a man was this close to the edge, a woman's best defense was serenity. "If you'll let me go, we'll talk. Would you like some coffee?"

His fingers tightened reflexively, then slowly relaxed. "You've bought a new pot."

"Yes." Was that humor in his eyes? she wondered. "There's only one chair. Why don't you use it while I go into the kitchen?"

He took her arm. "I don't want coffee, or a chair, or a pleasant conversation."

It seemed serenity wouldn't work. "All right, Stephen. What do you want?"

"You. I'd thought I'd made that fairly obvious." When she frowned, he glanced around the apartment. "Now tell me, Rebecca, is this what you want? A handful of rooms to be alone in?"

"I want to make the best of the rest of my life. I've already apologized for deceiving you. I realize that —"

"Deceiving me." He held up a finger to stop her. "I've wanted to clear that point up myself. How did you deceive me?"

"By letting you think that I was something I'm not."

"You're not a beautiful, interesting woman? A passionate woman?" He lifted a brow as he studied her. "Rebecca, I have too much pride to ever believe you could deceive me that completely."

He was confusing her — deliberately, she was sure. "I told you what I'd done."

"What you'd done," he agreed. "And how you'd done it." He brought his hand to her throat again, this time in a caress. His anger hadn't made her knees weak. She felt them tremble now at his tenderness. "Selling your possessions and flying to Paris for a new hairstyle. Quitting your job and grabbing life with both hands. You fascinate me." Her eyes stayed open wide when he brushed his lips over hers. "I think the time is nearly over when you'll be so easily flattered. It's almost a pity." He drew her closer, slowly, while his mouth touched hers. Relief coursed through him as he felt her melt and give. "Do you think it was your background that attracted me?"

"You were angry," she managed.

"Yes, angry at the idea that I had been part of your experiment. Furious," he added before he deepened the kiss. "Furious that I had been of only passing interest." She was heating in his arms, just as he remembered, just as he needed, softening, strengthening. "Shall I tell you how angry? Shall I tell you that for two weeks I couldn't work, couldn't think, couldn't function, because you were everywhere I looked and nowhere to be found?"

"I had to go." She was already tugging at his shirt to find the flesh beneath. To touch him again, just for a moment. To be touched by him. "When you said you regretted making love . . ." Her own words brought her back. Quickly she dropped her hands and stepped away.

He stared at her for a moment, then

abruptly swore and began to pace. "I've never thought myself this big a fool. I hurt you that night in a much different way than I'd believed. Then I handled it with less finesse than I might the most unimportant business transaction." He paused, sighing. For the first time she saw clearly how incredibly weary he was.

"You're tired. Please, sit down. Let me fix you something."

He took a moment to press his fingers to his eyes. Again he wanted to laugh — while he strangled her. She was exactly what he needed, what he understood. Yet at the same time she baffled him.

"You weaken me, Rebecca, and bring out the fool I'd forgotten I could be. I'm surprised you allowed me to set foot into your home. You should have —" As quickly as the anger had come, it faded. As quickly as the tension had formed, it eased. Everything he'd needed to see was in her eyes. Carefully now, he drew a deep breath. A man wasn't always handed so many chances at happiness.

"Rebecca, I never regretted making love with you." He stopped her from turning with the lightest of touches on her shoulder. "I regretted only the way it happened. Too much need and too little care.

I regret, I'll always regret, that for your first time there was fire but no warmth." He took her hands in his and brought them to his lips.

"It was beautiful."

"In its way." His fingers tightened on hers. Still so innocent, he thought. Still so generous. "It was not kind or patient or tender, as love should be the first time."

She felt hope rise in her heart again. "None of that mattered."

"It mattered, more than I can ever tell you. After, when you told me everything, it only mattered more. If I had done what my instincts told me to do that night you would never have left me. But I thought you needed time before you could bear to have me touch you again." Slowly, gently, he drew the tip of her finger into his mouth and watched her eyes cloud over. "Let me show you what I should have shown you then." With her hands locked in his, he looked into her eyes. "Do you want me?"

It was time for the truth. "Yes."

He lifted her into his arms and heard her breath catch. "Do you trust me?"

"Yes."

When he smiled, her heart turned over. "Rebecca, I must ask you one more thing."

"What is it?"

"Do you have a bed?"

She felt her cheeks heat even as she laughed. "In there."

She was trembling. It reminded him how careful he had to be, how precious this moment was to both of them. The sun washed over the bed, over them, as he lay beside her. And kissed her — only kissed her, softly, deeply, thoroughly, until her arms slipped from around him to fall bonelessly to her sides. She trembled still as he murmured to her, as his lips brushed over her cheeks, her throat.

He had shown her the desperation love could cause, the sharp-edged pleasure, the speed and the fury. Now he showed her that love could mean serenity and sweetness.

And she showed him.

He had thought to teach her, not to learn, to reassure her but not to be comforted. But he learned, and he was comforted. The need was there, as strong as it had been the first time. But strength was tempered with patience. As he slipped his hands down her robe to part it, to slide it away from her skin, he felt no need to hurry. He could delight in the way the sun slanted across her body, in the way her flesh warmed to his touch.

Her breath was as unsteady as her hands as she undressed him. But not from nerves. She understood that now. She felt strong and capable and certain. Anticipation made her tremble. Pleasure made her shudder. She gave a sigh that purred out of her lips as she arched against his seeking hands. Then he nipped lightly at her breast and she bounded from serenity to passion in one breathless leap.

Still he moved slowly, guiding her into a kind of heated torment she'd never experienced. Desire boiled in her, and his name sprang to her lips and her body coiled like a spring. Chaining down his own need, he set hers free and watched as she flew over the first peak.

"Only for me," he murmured as she went limp in his arms. "Only for me, Rebecca." With his own passions strapped, he slipped into her, determined to watch her build again. "Tell me you love me. Look at me and tell me."

She opened her eyes. She could barely breathe. Somehow the strength was pouring back into her, but so fast, so powerfully. Sensation rolled over sensation, impossibly. She moved with him, pressed center to center, heart to heart, but all she could see were his eyes, so dark, so blue, so intense. Perhaps she was drowning in them.

"I love you, Stephen."

Then she was falling, fathoms deep, into his eyes, into the sea. With her arms locked around him, she dragged him under with her.

He pulled her against him so that he could stroke her hair and wait for his pulse to level. She'd been innocent. But the surprise, the one he'd been dealing with for weeks, was that until Rebecca he'd been just as innocent. He'd known passion, but he'd never known intimacy, not the kind that reached the heart as fully as the body. And yet . . .

"We've been here before," he murmured. "Do you feel it, too?"

She linked her fingers with his. "I never believed in things like that until you. When I'm with you it's like remembering." She lifted her head to look at him. "I can't explain it."

"I love you, Rebecca, only more knowing who you are, why you are."

She touched a hand to his cheek. "I don't want you to say anything you don't really feel."

"How can a woman be so intelligent and

still so stupid?" With a shake of his head, Stephen rolled on top of her. "A man doesn't travel thousands of miles for this, however delightful it may be. I love you, and though it annoyed me for quite some time I'm accustomed to it now."

"Annoyed you."

"Infuriated." He kissed her to cut off whatever retort she might make. "I'd seen myself remaining free for years to come. Then I met a woman who sold her coffeepot so she could take pictures of goats."

"I certainly have no intention of interfering with your plans."

"You already have." He smiled, holding her still when she tried to struggle away. "Marriage blocks off certain freedoms and opens others."

"Marriage?" She stopped struggling but turned her head to avoid another kiss.

"Soon." He nuzzled her neck. "Immediately."

"I never said I'd marry you."

"No, but you will." With his fingertips only, he began to amuse her. "I'm a very persuasive man."

"I need to think." But she was trembling again. "Stephen, marriage is very serious."

"Deadly. And I should warn you that I've already decided to murder any man you look at for more than twenty seconds."

"Really?" She turned her head back, prepared to be angry. But he was smiling. No one else had ever smiled at her in quite that way. "Really?"

"I can't let you go, Rebecca. Can't and won't. Come back with me. Marry me. Have children with me."

"Stephen —"

He laid a finger to her lips. "I know what I'm asking you. You've already started a new life, made new plans. We've had only days together, but I can make you happy. I can promise to love you for a lifetime, or however many lifetimes we have. You once dived into the sea on impulse. Dive with me now, Rebecca. I swear you won't regret it."

Gently she pressed her lips to his fingertip, then drew his hand away. "All my life I've wondered what I might find if I had the courage to look. I found you, Stephen." With a laugh she threw her arms around him. "When do you want to leave?"